THE
WAR WITHIN

A Novel of the Civil War

D0973103

For Per

WITH LOVE AND THANKS . . .

First Aladdin Paperbacks edition September 2002
Text copyright © 2001 by Carol Matas

Aladdin Paperbacks
An imprint of Simon & Schuster
Children's Publishing Division
1230 Avenue of the Americas
New York, NY 10020

Also available in a Simon & Schuster Books for Young Readers hardcover edition.

The text of this book was set in 13-point Deepdene.

Printed in the United States of America
10 9 8 7 6 5 4 3

The Library of Congress has cataloged the hardcover edition as follows:

Matas, Carol, 1946–
The war within: a novel of the Civil War/by Carol Matas.
p.cm.
Summary: In 1862, after Union forces expel Hannah's family from Holly Springs, Mississippi, because they are Jews, Hannah reexamines her views regarding slavery and the war.

ISBN 0-689-82935-3 (hardcover)

1. United States—History—Civil War, 1861–1865—Juvenile Fiction. [1. United States—History—Civil War, 1861–1865—Fiction. 2. Jews—United States—Fiction. 3. Prejudices—Fiction. 4. Slavery—Fiction. 5. Mississippi—Fiction.] I. Title.
PZ7.M423964 War 2001
[Fic]—dc21   00-045068

ISBN 0-689-84358-5 (Aladdin pbk.)

THE
WAR WITHIN
A Novel of the Civil War

Written by
CAROL MATAS

ALADDIN PAPERBACKS
New York London Toronto Sydney Singapore

A NOTE FROM THE AUTHOR

Dear Reader,

I came across the story of the Jewish expulsion during the Civil War, quite by accident. I was reading about Judah P. Benjamin who was the Secretary of State for the Confederacy, thinking that perhaps I would write a play about him. He was Jewish and the highest ranking Jew to be in public office until Henry Kissinger over 100 years later. A book called Jews in the Civil War included a chapter about Ulysses S. Grant and his expulsion of Jews from the territories he controlled. This struck me as ironic since part of the motivation of the North was the freeing of slaves. How could they then justify discriminating against the Jews? It became even more interesting when I realized that Jews had owned slaves. Did they not see that they were practicing discrimination even as they railed against people discriminating against them? Had they forgotten that they celebrated their own escape from slavery every year at Passover?

What became the central question for me as I wrote this book was: How do we escape from the prisons that are our minds? We are brought up a certain way, with certain values. Some of us are brought up as Democrats, some Republicans. Some of us are brought up to believe in God, others as atheists. Some of us are brought up to be suspicious of everyone and everything; others are brought up to trust everyone and everything. As we grow up we are often encouraged to "think for ourselves." But how do we do that if we are so used to thinking in a certain way that we do not even realize we are doing it? Can any of us really say how we come to our decisions in life?

Hannah has been brought up to believe slavery is normal, even right. This book is about her journey, a journey inside herself as she begins to question her long-standing beliefs. What are your long-standing beliefs? Have you ever thought about it? Could you even recognize them or are they too ingrained? Can we learn to think for ourselves?

I try to keep one maxim in mind at all times. Hillel said, "What is hateful to you, do not do to your neighbor." Many people try to indoctrinate us with one way of thinking or another. But you can test it by using Hillel's advice. Had Hannah done that, she quickly would have realized that she would not want to be treated the way the slaves were treated.

I hope you have enjoyed this book and that it has given you something to think about. I'll always be glad to hear your thoughts. You can e-mail me at carol@carolmatas.com.

ACKNOWLEDGMENTS

First and foremost, I would like to thank my researcher, Lisa Grant. She worked not only tirelessly, but also with a fantastic enthusiasm for the topic, and with a plain old love for pure research. Dr. Jonathan Sarna, chair of the Near Eastern and Judaic Studies Department of Brandeis University, pointed Lisa in the right direction; Dr. Mark Greenberg, resident historian at the Museum of the Southern Jewish Experience, talked to me early on in the process, giving me an important overview of the Southern Jewish experience. Also, thank you to Leah Berkowitz, who was so generous with information and advice. (If there are any mistakes, none of these esteemed scholars are responsible.)

Thanks to my editor, David Gale, and his assistant, John Rudolph, at Simon & Schuster, and to my editor, Diane Kerner, at Scholastic Canada.

I used the Web extensively and would like to send out a blanket thank-you to all those who have worked so hard and have developed maps, photos, and descriptions of everything from clothes to the psalms that were sung at that time.

Perry Nodelman gave me invaluable critiques, as always. And my husband, Per Brask, listened chapter by chapter and gave me much-needed support through the entire process.

For Per

WITH LOVE AND THANKS . . .

Prologue

December 26, 1862

The war has changed everything. And it has changed me.

As I sit here on this boat, staring at the mighty Mississippi River clogged with steamers transporting troops and supplies, I cannot help but contemplate the past ten days. Ten days ago I knew what was important: order, decorum, manners, etiquette. That is what it meant to be a Southern lady. And that was the task I was concentrating on—fashioning myself from a girl into a woman.

I have managed to find myself a small corner, where I am hiding away from the sights and smells of this hospital ship, and I have been rereading my diary. I do not recognize the person I was.

How is that possible? And yet, considering what has occurred, how is it *not* possible? The diary ends on the sixteenth of December. I had no time or opportunity to write in it after that. Perhaps, though, if I think back over what has transpired over these last ten days, I could try to make some sense of it. I must make sense of it, I *must*.

I remember I was distraught because of a doll. How silly that seems now. A doll!

I walked into my room to find my favorite porcelain doll lying on its side on the floor.

"Not Elizabeth," I exclaimed aloud, although there was no one there to hear me. I rushed over to see if she was broken. I picked her up gingerly and found, to my great relief, that she was still in one piece. Jule, my servant, was cleaning my sister Joanna's room, next to mine. I summoned her immediately.

"You know, Jule," I said in my sternest voice, "that I do not enjoy reprimanding you."

"Yes, Miss Hannah." Although her words were meek, she did not appear to be particularly worried. I had to make it clear to her that I was the mistress and that she had to pay attention to me. I was a child no longer.

"I cannot tolerate such things," I warned her. "My doll could easily break if treated in this heartless manner."

"Missy," Jule replied, eyes to the floor, "I swear I put it up proper. Now your little brother David, he be in here earlier. I don't like to tell no tales, missy, but if I was you, I'd look to your diary."

Horrified, I followed Jule's pointing finger. Of course, I always put my diary behind my dolls. Why that little . . . !

I drew myself up with as much dignity as I could muster. "I am sorry, Jule, I know you are always careful with my things. Please excuse my bad temper."

Recently my dear friend Eugenia had pointed out to

me that I was far too familiar with our slaves and I had resolved to change. I turned away to look for my younger brother, feeling both confused and a little ashamed by my sternness with Jule. Eugenia was right, of course, but then why did I feel so uncomfortable?

Jule gave me an inscrutable look out of the corner of her eye and went about her work. I immediately determined to find my younger brother David and to scold him mercilessly. I was so angry I began to run out of my room, but hearing Ma's voice in my head, I slowed down. Naturally, I had been reminded over and over by Ma that young ladies, unlike girls, never run. At long last, on my thirteenth birthday, which I had celebrated only a month earlier, I had been allowed to wear a three-hoop crinoline instead of the babyish two-hoop variety, which *proved* that I was now a young lady.

I was proud of my new status and I was trying terribly hard to behave with appropriate dignity—which wasn't easy in this instance, with my brother provoking me in this manner. That little devil had been making my life a misery from morning until night. But my diary! That really was beyond anything and everything! Why, I would thrash him! Yes, he deserved it and he'd be sorry.

"Hannah?" Ma was climbing the stairs, slowly, as if she were too tired to make it to the landing. "Hannah, slow yourself down, I must speak to you."

"Yes, Ma," I answered, reluctant to stop even for a moment.

"You must go take over in the store for me, dear. I've

been there since five this morning and I am so tired, I need to rest."

I tried not to show my displeasure. It was bad enough that those dreadful, hateful, brutish Yanks had thrown all of us children out of our schools so that they could use the buildings for storing guns or food or whatever other endless supplies with which they kept filling up the town . . . but now my lessons at home were constantly being interrupted by work in the store.

"Isn't Joanna there?" I asked. "Or Henry?"

"Why, yes, but your sister can't manage alone; and your brother had to make a delivery to Mrs. Grant, so he won't be back for a bit. Go on, now."

Well, that just took the cake! It *would* be the Yankee general's wife who was the cause of my having to go and work in the store. Still, I had more important things to discuss with Ma, namely the little troublemaker.

"Ma," I said, "David has been reading in my diary!"

"Hannah," Ma answered in a weary tone, "please do not trouble me with such things. If you would take him in hand as I have so often asked, he would not get into so much trouble."

"But, Ma, I cannot roughhouse with him; I cannot play with him in a way that would help him get rid of all the energy he has. That is a boy's job. And with Pa and Simon and Leon away, surely it is Henry you should be speaking to about this, not me!" I was indignant. How on earth did this end up as *my* fault?

"You well know that Henry is much too busy in the store to watch David. I have told you, Hannah, that you must take on more responsibility." She sighed. "I am far too fatigued to have this discussion with you now, and Joanna needs help immediately." With that, she continued to her room with no thought whatsoever to David's obvious misdeeds.

Despite my preoccupation with young David, as I walked down the stairs I held my head high and tried not to look down, practicing the graceful descent in my new hoops, and imagining a fine young gentleman gazing up at me adoringly as I floated elegantly toward him. When I gained the foyer, instead of a handsome young admirer it was David's voice that surprised me out of my daydream.

"Hannah, Hannah, may I come with you? Where are you going?"

I whirled around and glared at him. He was tall for his age of seven years, and thin. His eyes were as big as saucers and as blue as a midsummer sky; they seemed to be the only thing you could see when you looked at the boy. He was so adorable, one glance and my heart always melted. But I reminded myself that his behavior had not been that of a gentleman, and that even if no one else in the household cared, I would have to teach him right from wrong.

"David, did you read my diary?"

"Well now, Hannah," David replied, "I'm not so sure how to answer that."

"Explain yourself, young man," I ordered.

"The thing is," he said, his eyes shifting away, "I was bored and I went looking for you and you weren't there.

And I needed someone to talk to so bad, and yet, your *diary* was there and that's a kind of talking, isn't it?" He looked up at me to see if his words were having the desired effect.

They were not. "Yes, it is me talking to my diary, *privately*. And you well know that! So you, David, you will come with me to the store, and you will fetch and carry for me the entire day!"

"Thank you, Sister!" David replied, his eyes lighting up.

"This is a *punishment*," I exclaimed, exasperated.

"I know, I know!" David said, beaming from ear to ear.

I sighed. "Where is Jule?" I turned and called, "Jule? Jule?"

Jule came running. "Yes, missy?"

"Please dress Master David. He is accompanying me to the store."

It was cold out and looked like it would rain any second. Our house, on the south side of the town square, was about a five-minute walk from the store, which was catty-corner to the other side of the square. I put on my coat, pulled an umbrella out of the stand, just in case, and pulled on my gloves. It took some time before Jule managed to get David bundled up, but finally, holding tightly to his hand, I took a deep breath and stepped out the door.

It was a shock, as always, to see how the Yanks had spoiled our town. Our house stood on one of the most beautiful streets in Holly Springs, but I hardly recognized anything anymore and I hated walking out-of-doors. As long as I was inside our beautiful and elegant home, everything was orderly and controlled (and if it wasn't, I made certain it was). Outside, though, one never knew what one might encounter.

I pulled David along behind me as we walked quickly to the store. We had to step carefully, however, because the streets were filled with barrels of flour and bales of cotton. Yankees on their horses hurtled this way and that with no thought for those walking, so between the supplies and their mounts there was hardly room for a citizen to move.

I always loved to gaze at the houses whenever I went to the store—two- and three-story homes, covered in Virginia creeper, many made from red brick, with Victorian gables up high and elaborate ironwork on the front verandas. In the spring and early summer the magnolias and the white-blossomed Kwansan cherry trees would flower, and the scent would be enough to make any young lady swoon. On the other side of the street red and yellow tulips and white and yellow daffodils were planted all around the town square, shaded by white pines and Atlas cedars, and white and red oaks. Inside the town square the big buildings that used to house the law and government offices for our town were now bursting at the seams with medical supplies, sutlers' goods (clothing and uniforms), and guns and munitions. I gazed up at the old four-faced clock tower, the only thing undisturbed by the Yanks, and tried to put my focus on it, disregarding the intruders around me.

"Hannah, Hannah," David shouted, "watch out!"

I almost walked right into a large bale of cotton. However hard I tried, I couldn't ignore my surroundings. I remembered the peaceful beauty that had existed before General Grant took over Holly Springs in the middle of November to use it as a storage facility, a staging place for his planned attack on Vicksburg, and the memory made me long for those days.

We reached the store without further incident, and I paused outside for a moment to admire my handiwork.

"It looks mighty fine," David said as he stared at the window display.

"Thank you, David." I smiled, finally forgiving him for his bad behavior earlier. I'd worked so hard on the Christmas display—I only wished Pa could see it. In the center of the window was a metal toy train; beside it was a little toy drum, and just behind that were toy soldiers. Then I had made two displays for girls—one of beautiful porcelain dolls, the other of intricately designed music boxes.

When we walked into the shop I felt the welcome blast of warm air from the big potbellied stove in the center of the room. The store was packed with customers, but as I looked around I quickly realized that no one was helping them. Joanna was, in fact, ignoring them all because she was talking to Captain Mazer!

I could feel my cheeks turn red, I was so incensed. A Federal officer! And my sister, Joanna, apparently mesmerized by the young gentleman, completely under his spell! Ever since he had walked into the store in November with greetings from our uncle Jacob in Cincinnati, a neighbor of the captain's, Joanna had been hopeless. And Ma had been just as bad, treating him as if he were a normal boy. Why, he was a Yankee!

"He's an Israelite," Ma would say. "He's one of us, and he's lonesome. Would you not want a family to take care of Simon or Leon?" I would, of course, but Simon and Leon were handsome young gentlemen. Who would not want them in their home?

I examined Captain Mazer as I took off my bonnet. He was handsome, I had to admit, with fine whiskers and a shock of black hair. Tall, with broad shoulders and gray eyes, he cut quite a figure in his uniform. But how could Joanna look at that uniform every day and not become queasy? And she was ignoring the other customers, who were testy at the best of times these days since there was a different shortage each day—either flour or sugar or salt. People still demanded coffee, too, even though it had become as scarce as a fresh peach in December.

I hurried to the counter and with a curt nod greeted Captain Mazer and Joanna.

Joanna, her cheeks aglow, didn't seem to notice my disapproval. "Hannah! I've just invited Captain Mazer to our Chanukah party tonight. He's accepted and is bringing his dear friend Mr. Katz."

I tried to be polite and not make a face. Mr. Katz—Private Katz—was the most accident-prone individual I had ever met. Why, the man could trip over his own two feet!

At the same time, I couldn't believe I had temporarily

forgotten about Chanukah. It must have been that business with my diary. It had wiped everything else from my memory. Still, there was not too much to do. Ma had long ago trained our cook, Emily, to make potato pancakes. And, of course, we would play dreidel games and eat chocolate.

I felt better. Even with Yankees in the house there would still be a party, things would proceed as they had every year. We would light the menorah and some feeling of order would return. I smoothed my skirt and then looked around the crowded shop. Where to begin?

, , ,

Joanna wore her new gown that night, a blue silk dress with three-quarter sleeves that matched the blue of her eyes exactly. I had put artificial flowers in her black hair and her creamy skin glowed with good health. She looked radiant. I was such an ugly goose in comparison to her. I did put on my cream tulle, however, and thought I was as presentable as I could be. Normally Captain Mazer complimented both of us, as well as Ma, on our looks, but that night, despite Joanna's extra efforts (and mine), he said nothing. He seemed preoccupied right from the start of the evening. For instance, Private Katz tripped on the doorstep on his way in, and Captain Mazer would normally have teased him mercilessly. Instead he seemed not to even notice.

The potato pancakes were delicious. Because Captain Mazer was so inattentive, Private Katz tried to keep the conversation alive.

"What do you hear, ma'am," he asked, "of your sons and your husband?"

"We have had letters," Ma answered, "from Simon and from my dear husband, but have heard nothing from our Leon since he left here in October."

I glared at Private Katz. How dare he ask about our family, as if he cared—wasn't it due to his Union army that our men were in danger? It's true Pa wasn't fighting; he had been appointed chief commissary for the troops of Mississippi. Somehow he had to find food, medicine, uniforms, and shoes for the troops, which wasn't easy because of the Federal blockade. He always tried to cheer us up, though, by reminding us that while he obtained supplies for the army, he was able to obtain supplies for the store as well. We had the best-stocked store in town. But Ma scoffed at such thinking. She just wanted him home, as did we all.

"I hope, ma'am," the private said, "that you will have good news of him soon."

And I hope, I thought, *that he is at this moment killing many of your compatriots.* Naturally I could voice no such thought. I would be regarded as bloodthirsty and unladylike.

"Simon is rough!" David declared, speaking to Private Katz. "He's rough!" he repeated with pride.

Ma smiled. "Our eldest, Simon," she explained, "is with the Barksdale's Mississippians. Their nickname is the Rough and Readies."

"Ready to shoot Yanks!" David exclaimed.

"David!" Joanna reprimanded him. "Please do not be rude to our guests. I am sure you are aware that they are Union."

I tried not to laugh aloud. Good for David!

"'Course I am, Sister," David said, shaking his head. "Look at their uniforms. I ain't a baby."

"I am not a baby," Ma corrected him.

"Leon was at military academy," David continued, ignoring Ma's interruption. "He always got into trouble."

Ma laughed. "David, you do remember the funniest things." She thought for a minute. "Let me see if I can recall all his infractions. I believe he was cited for throwing spitballs, skylarking at mess, laughing at exercise, and being disorderly at drill."

"Do not forget," Joanna added, "being noisy in the study room and having his musket out of order."

I had to add my laughter to theirs. Leon was always in trouble. He had signed up just this summer at age sixteen, against Ma's wishes. And no doubt he was keeping his entire regiment in stitches.

After our meal we moved to the front parlor, where we played the dreidel game. We each bet with pecans supplied by Henry from the store. I spun and the dreidel fell on *halb*, so I got half the pot. Joanna spun next and got a *shtel*, so she had to add three pecans, which was the ante. Ma spun a *nichts*, as did Private Katz, so they got nothing. Captain Mazer spun a *shtel*, as Joanna had, and for some reason the two of them found it humorous that they had spun the exact same thing. Finally it was David's turn—and he spun a *ganz*, winning the whole thing!

"I win. I win!" he exclaimed. "Can I eat them, Ma?"

Ma smiled and nodded. She knew how terribly

David missed his pa and his brothers, and was just pleased to see him happy.

Jule brought in the tea and the chocolate. Ma served everyone, and at that point Captain Mazer seemed to come to life. He turned a deep red and cleared his throat.

"I have had some very bad news today," he said, turning to address Ma.

"And what is that, sir?" she replied, obviously concerned.

He stood then and cleared his throat again. "There has been profiteering in cotton in this area, as you know," he said.

Ma looked puzzled. "Yes, of course I know."

We all did. Pa always told us how carefully he priced everything, so as never to take advantage of the war to make excess profit.

Captain Mazer seemed unable to continue.

Private Katz took pity on him. He rose to talk and immediately tripped over his own foot. He would have tumbled onto the floor had Captain Mazer not shot out his hand and caught him in the nick of time. Once upright, he began to talk in the speedy way he had.

"General Grant's dad, Jesse, he's in business with a Jewish man. And I hear they got into a big fight with the general, wanting special treatment to buy and sell cotton. And General Grant got so mad, what with all the profiteering that's going on already, well, he's made an order for the Department of the Tennessee, which is all the land hereabouts in Mississippi and into Tennessee and Kentucky, that all Jews must be expelled from these territories within twenty-four hours of the order. That is, twenty-four hours as of today."

Ma looked blank. "I don't understand," she said.

"He blames the Jews for trading in cotton. He wants them out."

"But we live here," Ma said, still not comprehending.

Henry spoke up then. "It isn't true!" he exclaimed. "The Jews aren't involved—no more than anyone. Why, it's mostly the *army* that's doing it. I see it all the time."

Joanna had turned pale and could not seem to speak. I tried to make sense of it all but was unable to.

"I know it is not true," Captain Mazer said. "I am ashamed to be part of an army that would issue such an iniquitous order, and I want you to know that I for one will do what I can to protect you. *I* won't send you away, that is for certain. The townsfolk depend on you. They don't see you as different because you are Israelites, and I am sure they will not give you away. And with your last name, Green, why, it isn't obvious, is it, that you *are* Israelites—I mean, to the Union troops. I am sure it will all blow over."

"Do you mean to say," Joanna said slowly, "that we are to be thrown out of our house and sent away because we are Jews?"

There was a long, horrible pause.

"Not if I can help it," Captain Mazer said quietly.

Suddenly I understood. Suddenly I realized what we could be facing.

"And you," I said, standing up, "you Yankees lecture

us on equality. You lecture us about our slaves! Yet you would stand by and let this happen?"

Captain Mazer couldn't seem to answer. After an awkward pause he bowed, and thanked Ma for her hospitality. Then, along with Private Katz, he withdrew, leaving us to try to comprehend what we had just been told. I sank back into my chair, a feeling of dread washing over me. Could this happen? And if it did, what could be worse?

I awoke the next morning feeling terrible. I had been so upset the night before that I had been unable to sleep. Ma had given me some Kopp's Baby Friend syrup, which had had the effect of knocking me unconscious rather than helping me sleep. I was groggy and my head hurt.

Jule came into the room and served me a strong cup of tea with lots of sugar in it. As I sipped it, slowly my head began to clear.

"Miss Hannah," Jule said, "you ain't forgot you supposed to be over at Miss Eugenia's house today, have you?"

I almost dropped my teacup. "Of course I'd forgotten!" I exclaimed. "My head feels like it's full of cotton wool, Jule. Oh, my heavens! Help me get ready!"

"What you want to wear today, Miss Hannah? It's cold and damp out there."

"I shall wear my dark blue poplin, Jule, and you can put out the matching toque and muff, please, if it is that chill outside."

"Yes, missy."

"And please give the box of materials I put together yesterday to Moses."

"Yes, missy, I'll have Moses put them in the gig."

I put down my cup and dragged myself out of bed. Eugenia could be very stern, almost like a schoolmarm, if she was displeased. I did *not* want to be late. Today, after all, my friends and myself had been given a huge responsibility—the decorations for the ball of the season to be held at Eugenia's mansion the following night.

My girlfriends and I had been looking forward to the ball for weeks. Eugenia's pa, as owner of the largest bank in town, would not let the Yanks spoil a town tradition. That's what he had said to us only a week ago.

As I washed my face with the warm water Jule poured into the washstand I began to feel better. I sponged myself all over, and that also helped to wake me up. Every time the thought of what Captain Mazer had said came into my head, I resolutely pushed it out.

I will not consider it, I thought. *It simply proves what barbarians the Yanks are. Fortunately Captain Mazer has offered to protect us, and I refuse to give such nonsense any more credence!*

I had to repeat this over and over to myself as Jule fixed my hair, because the nasty words of last night kept returning to haunt me. And I found it difficult to think clearly about Captain Mazer. Was he not a hated Yank? And yet he was behaving almost like a Southern gentleman.

"Stop shakin' your head like that, Miss Hannah," Jule scolded me. "How you 'spect me to do your braids? You can't get bad thoughts out by shakin' 'em out, you know."

I took a deep breath and tried to sit still, but it wasn't easy. I hoped Ma would be able to contact Pa—he would know what to do. But what if she couldn't?

I was finally dressed and ready to go.

"Now, Miss Hannah, you ain't runnin' off without your breakfast," Jule said sternly. "You'll just get all dizzy again, won't you?"

"But I cannot be late!" I objected.

"Get some food down you first," Jule warned. I knew what that tone meant. It meant or else she'd have to tell Ma. I considered being stern right back, as I had been with her the day before, but I was in a rush and I decided that such a conversation would only slow me down. I didn't want to admit to myself how unpleasant I had found scolding Jule, and in a way I was used to her fussing over me. So, meekly I hurried downstairs for breakfast.

I was walking toward the morning room when I heard voices in the front parlor. Curious, I slipped quietly along the hallway until I was standing just outside the door. It was the mayor's wife, Mrs. Foster. Her voice was unmistakable—she shouted everything at the top of her lungs.

"But, Clara, my dear," she was saying to Ma, "you are not the Jews General Grant is referring to. *You* are different. He refers to those Jews who profiteer. He cannot mean for you and your family to leave!"

Ma answered anxiously, "I hope you are right, Elizabeth, but he did name all Jews, as a class."

Mrs. Foster clicked her tongue in disapproval. "I am sure Mrs. Grant is simply too put out with him. Wait until he returns! She'll give him a piece of her mind, I declare!"

"I have found her to be so gracious," Ma said. "Really a lovely person."

"Well, she is for a Yank, I'll give her that. She has behaved most proper living in the Walters' house. And she has manners." I heard Mrs. Foster's skirts rustle as she rose. "Now, you mustn't worry. We simply won't let them make you leave."

I could hear that Ma was crying. "Thank you, Elizabeth. A true friend is someone who is there for you in time of trouble." She paused. "How are your boys?"

The Fosters had lost a son at the start of the war and now had three other boys fighting.

"Praise God, still alive," Mrs. Foster answered. "And yours?"

"We have not heard a word from Leon for far too long."

"If he had been killed," Mrs. Foster reminded her, "you would have read it in the newspaper lists."

"Perhaps he's ill. That is my concern," Ma answered. "Why, we seem to be losing more boys to sicknesses than to the fighting."

"He is a strong lad, though, is he not?" Mrs. Foster said in an encouraging tone.

When I heard Mrs. Foster moving toward the open parlor door I quickly hurried down the hall and into the morning room. Only David was there when I entered. Joanna and Henry must have already eaten.

"Are we going to have to leave our house?" David asked, wide-eyed. "Last night Ma said we might have to go to Uncle Jacob in Cincinnati."

"Nonsense," I said to him. "I've just heard Ma talking with Mrs. Foster. No one wants us to leave, and we are not going anywhere."

"Good," David said, grinning, "because Pa said I could have a horse next year, and I bet I couldn't get one in Cincinnati." He was gobbling down huge mouthfuls of eggs and griddle cakes as he spoke. "Ma would scold you proper if she knew you'd been listening outside the door," he added. "She's always scolding *me* about it!"

"Well, she doesn't know, and she won't know, will she?" I warned David as I helped myself to some griddle cakes and forced myself to eat at least a few bites. "Now, you behave while I'm gone today, David," I added. "Try not to get into trouble."

"But what can I do?"

"You can study your lessons after Miss Douglas leaves, that's what. I've told her already that I'll be back in the classroom tomorrow."

David looked as if I'd just sentenced him to five years in prison. I had to hide a small giggle as I said good-bye. I went to the front door and waited for the gig to pull around to the front of the house.

It was too far to walk to Eugenia's in the chill weather, so Ma had arranged for our servant Moses to drive me. Mrs. Foster's brougham pulled away as our gig pulled up. Just as I was about to leave, Ma caught me at the door and gave me a hug and a kiss.

"I think all will be well," Ma said. "Try not to worry. How is your head, dear?"

"Getting clearer, thank you, Ma," I answered. "It was kind of Mrs. Foster to pay you a visit."

"Wasn't it?" Ma said, dabbing at her eyes with a handkerchief. "Now, there's Moses, so off you go!"

, , ,

Eugenia greeted me at the door and led me to the back parlor. She was wearing a stunning morning dress of lilac faille and had her long black hair done in perfect ringlets with fresh flowers braided through them. She always wore fresh flowers in her hair no matter what the season or what the cost! Her cheeks were pink and glowing as always. In fact, with my black hair and fair skin I could have been her sister, except that I had the large blue eyes of all the Green family, whereas Eugenia's were a deep brown.

Moses put the heavy box down and bowed out of the room.

"Thank you, Moses," I called after him.

"Why, Hannah dear," Eugenia said sweetly, "you look quite peaky today. Whatever is the matter?"

I almost blurted everything out, but my pride restrained me. I was afraid that Eugenia would think less of me. I worried that Eugenia would suddenly see me as different, an outsider, because of my Jewish background. We had always kept our Jewishness to ourselves. Pa would explain that it was important for us to be the same as everyone else. He never wanted us to be singled out the way Jews were in the old country. So we made our observances at home, and when we were with our neighbors, we celebrated as they did, and it all seemed to work admirably.

"You must sit down, dear," Eugenia commiserated. "I'll tell Poppie to make you some tea." I sank into a chair and tried to regain my composure as Eugenia left me alone for a moment. I was convinced that ignoring the entire subject would somehow make it disappear, and that is what I resolved to do.

Eugenia bustled back into the room, followed by Mary and Claudia. Mary looked pretty as ever dressed in a skirt, a fine white muslin blouse, and a large Swiss belt. Her blond hair was done in so many elaborate braids her maid must have worked for an hour straight, but Mary always felt it was time worth taking. She was complaining about the drive into town as she kissed my cheek.

"I declare," she exclaimed, "we were delayed almost an hour by a column of Yanks walking ahead of the carriage. But thank the good Lord, they left our plantation alone."

Claudia followed her in, dressed as always in a plain woolen camp dress, her brown hair plaited in one braid. Eugenia used to whisper to me, "You'd never know her pa is a banker. I swear he acts more like a missionary. And the way they make her dress! Poor thing, what a cross to bear. How will she ever find a man that way?"

Poppie placed a tray full of tea and cakes on one of the small, round tables in the room, and the others dug in to the food with great appreciation. I found that my appetite had disappeared altogether.

"My new white silk was finished yesterday," Mary said, smiling. "Mrs. Latham has quite outdone herself this time."

"Oh, you are fortunate," Eugenia said. "Ma says I must make do with my pink silk, as I've worn it only once and she has other things to spend her money on, namely our fighting boys." Eugenia sighed. "I know she's right, but I have found the most divine pattern and Mrs. Latham agrees it will suit me admirably. On the other hand," she continued, "with all the boys and men away who will be there to admire us?" She turned to me. "What will you wear, Hannah?"

"An old dress of Joanna's." I sighed, echoing Eugenia. "A sky blue tulle. Although I have been working on it and I've added a sash of white ribbon and white satin ruchings. I think it will do."

We did not bother to ask Claudia what she would wear, as it was bound to be something dreadful. Yet she seemed oblivious to such concerns.

"Enough of this, girls," Eugenia said. "We must get to work. Hannah, you have some color returning to your cheeks. No doubt a little enterprise will help put us all in good color."

She pulled out the strips of fabric, colored paper, and ribbons from the boxes. We were allowed to touch only the ballroom. The dining room would naturally have flowers and ice sculptures—Eugenia's mother was in charge of all that.

"I suggest we drape this fabric along the walls," Eugenia said.

"We could tack it up with sprigs of holly," I proposed.

"An excellent idea," Eugenia said with approval. I began to feel better.

"And the colored paper can festoon the punch table," Mary added.

"These ribbons can go on the punch table and the

walls," Claudia suggested. "I do hope those Northern louts will realize that the Confederate blue and gray we have chosen as our theme colors are chosen for a reason."

"I am sure it will not be lost on them," Mary assured her.

"Let us waste no more time," Eugenia declared. "We shall put our plans into action!" And with that dramatic statement she led the way into the ballroom. Her servant Zacharia carried the boxes for us and remained to help us put up fabric and ribbons where it was too high for us to reach.

We worked all morning until the room looked quite festive. Poppie came in when we were almost done and extended an invitation from Eugenia's ma for us all to stay for dinner. We were quite famished by then, myself included. The work and the companionship of my friends had allowed me to forget almost completely the unpleasantness of the night before, and I was once again feeling cheerful and happy—what I considered to be my natural state.

As we sat down in the dining room to eat, Mrs. Hunter could hardly contain herself. "Girls," she said, "can you keep a secret?"

We all nodded yes.

"Aloud," she demanded.

"Yes, *ma'am*," we answered in unison. My heart sank a little. I had never liked secrets; I was in the habit of confiding almost all things to either Joanna or Henry, depending on which one I felt could best manage that particular confidence. For example, anything of a womanly nature I discussed with Joanna, whereas any thoughts on the war were more naturally shared with Henry. Once I had sworn, however, I knew that I was honor bound never to breathe a word. Something, I thought, those Yanks would never understand. Honor.

"Well, then," Mrs. Hunter said. "It is a secret we will share with only the women of Holly Springs. And not with those who might have friends in the Union army." She glanced pointedly at me. Joanna! Her friendship with Captain Mazer was the talk of the town obviously! Oh, I could have strangled her. I was mortified.

"I have heard from Mr. Hunter that our boys are close. Very close. We may expect to be rescued from these Yanks at any moment!"

We all let loose a spontaneous shriek of delight. Why, this news was too good to be true!

"And," she continued, "in case it is very soon—for instance, the day after tomorrow, as the rumor goes—we have a special duty to make sure all those nice Federal officers come to the ball. It is possible, young ladies, that our ball will be the Union's downfall! We know that General Grant is depending on the supplies he is storing here in town to feed his army as they march to Vicksburg. And if he doesn't take Vicksburg it will be a big victory for the South!

"I will be putting one hundred-proof liquor in the punch. Now, you girls will be behind the table serving the punch. You must call the boys over and serve them again and again. Talk with them and refill their glasses while you talk. The older girls will dance them off their feet to work up a thirst!" She rubbed her hands. "It is simply too perfect! If our boys arrive on schedule, the Federals will be too weak from drink to resist!"

I felt quite overcome. Never in my wildest dreams had I thought that I, a mere girl, could have any effect on the war. All girls could do was sit at home and wait. Although Ma often said that the sewing we did and the money we helped to raise through balls and socials were what kept their army going, it hardly seemed enough. The thrill of the news, added to our hard work of the morning, gave me an excellent appetite, and I devoured the roasted quail with unqualified delight.

After lunch the four of us girls huddled together in the back parlor, holding hands.

"Our boys could be back," I sighed. "Why, Leon or Simon could be with them—who knows? I wonder which regiments are coming. Maybe they'll push the Yanks all the way back to Washington!"

"I'd be happy simply to see them out of Holly Springs," Eugenia said. "Would it not be lovely to have our streets back to ourselves?"

"The sooner they leave the better for Joanna," I confided to my friends. "Once Captain Mazer is no longer here, she'll set her sights on a more suitable young man."

"I always thought she'd marry my brother," Mary said. "I think George has always hoped for the same."

"Then first we must rid ourselves of the captain," I said decisively.

"I hope our boys rip those Yanks limb from limb," Claudia said, smiling. She'd always had a liking for the macabre, which made me a bit uncomfortable. And her words suddenly gave me a twinge of conscience. Joanna did seem genuinely fond of Captain Mazer. And he *was* an Israelite, as Ma had pointed out. It wouldn't be very nice if *he* were to be ripped limb from limb. And yet I couldn't warn him, could I? First of all, I had sworn an oath, and an oath could never be broken. Secondly, he'd be honor bound (if the Yanks had such a thing) to tell his superiors, and then the surprise raid would surely fail. No, I would have to remain quiet.

, , ,

"Ma," Joanna said at the supper table that night, "I have something to tell you."

"I hope," I interjected, "you are about to inform us that you have discouraged Captain Mazer from showing you any more attention. It is being noticed by all our friends."

Joanna flushed in anger and glared at me. "Quite the opposite!" she declared. "Captain Mazer wishes to speak to Pa."

"You are going to marry a Yank!" I could not believe my ears. "But what about George, Mary's brother?"

"George?" Joanna thought for a moment. "Why, he's a fine boy. He simply isn't Jonathan."

"I think Captain Mazer is a good young man," Ma said. "After all, Hannah, Pa's brother and all your cousins are for the Union. Does that make them bad people?"

I forced myself to bite my tongue. I wanted to blurt out, "Yes!" Wasn't it obvious? They were killing our boys. Even now who knew how Leon, Simon, or Pa could be suffering. And every single boy or young man was away or about to go away, or home in the ground. The Yanks were the enemy! It took a great effort for me to stay silent at that moment, but I knew that if I spoke my mind I would only provoke Joanna and Ma. They were too blind to see the truth.

I smiled to myself. Soon—soon the Yanks would be gone. I could afford to keep silent. I didn't need to argue. Captain Mazer and that silly Private Katz wouldn't be here much longer! And I, little Hannah Green, was about to help defeat them!

December 19, 1862

The next morning I felt almost feverish from excitement. The ball was so close and perhaps the Yankee defeat would follow right upon its heels. I dressed quickly without even calling Jule to help me and sat at the desk in my room, conjugating French verbs in preparation for my lessons with Miss Douglas. I tried desperately to take my mind off what was about to happen. Finally, later that morning, Miss Douglas arrived and we met in the morning room.

"Miss Green," Miss Douglas said as she patted her gray hair down, "you are making very good progress. I can see that you are working well on your own, something, I am afraid, not all the young ladies I have the privilege to teach are able to manage. I fail to understand how the Union can justify taking all our schools away from us. Can they not store their precious goods in tents or some such thing? I must admit to you, Miss Green, that I am not as young as I once was, and traveling from house to house like this giving lessons is quite wearing me out!"

"Maybe it will not be for much longer," I said, wishing desperately that I could tell her the truth and give her hope.

"Or maybe it will be for years longer," she sighed. "Your mother and Mrs. Hunter are looking into rotating classes from home to home, and I think that would make it easier on us teachers who are at present running all over the town going from one student to the next."

I was simply bursting to tell her that as of tomorrow we might be back in school, but somehow I managed not to say anything.

"Have you read any more in Miss Austen's *Pride and Prejudice*?" she asked me, moving on to our study of literature.

"I have," I answered. "Do you think the title word *pride* refers to Mr. Darcy or to Miss Bennet?"

"I must ask you what you think," she answered.

"I admit to being confused by the issue," I responded. "On the surface it seems that the pride is all on Mr. Darcy's part, but as the book progresses one cannot but wonder if Miss Bennet is not stubborn and prideful herself. She cannot see his excellent qualities; she only sees what appearances suggest."

"I would say that is an excellent analysis." Miss Douglas smiled, obviously pleased. "You must always examine as deep as you can into a text, and you will hopefully discover that which is beneath the surface. Things are not always as they appear."

How true, I thought. *At this moment you believe this to be an ordinary day like any other, when by tomorrow our lives might be completely altered.* I wondered if God looked down on us in such a way—shaking His head at our ignorance of what was to come. And then I wondered what made me think of God. With Pa not home to teach us our Jewish history lessons and our catechism, God was rarely spoken of in the house. Ma worried about practical issues; she had no time for discussions of heavenly things.

"Miss Green, you seem to have wandered off in your

mind," Miss Douglas said gently. "I suggest you read further in your book while I put David through his mathematics lessons." As I was leaving the room David entered. He made a very funny face as he passed me, which he hid nicely from Miss Douglas but which sent me into a fit of giggles.

I quickly found myself immersed in my book, too immersed, in fact. Much to my horror I suddenly realized I had finished the entire thing and was left with nothing else to do. The spell of the story was too much with me to wish for another novel to take its place right away. I felt at a loss and even began to consider going to help at the store to take my mind off waiting. Normally I tried to stay away from working in the store—it was so unladylike, a fact Eugenia enjoyed pointing out to me as often as possible. But with Pa, Simon, and Leon away, women had to work. It was happening everywhere in the town.

Before I could leave, a note was delivered to me from Mary. I was invited to the plantation for the afternoon for tea and to do needlework. I was thrilled. Mary had sent her buggy and servant, so I told Jule to inform Ma where I had gone. Taking my cape, I hurried out to the carriage.

The weather had cleared. It was cool but dry, and the drive of approximately twenty minutes was lovely. There were few signs of war on the quiet back road, lined with pine trees and dogwoods, and few signs of the Federals, too. They had left the plantations alone, for the moment, concentrating all their resources in the town. The road to Memphis, or to Jackson, that would have been different—full of troops, no doubt.

It was blissfully quiet on the road. I hadn't realized how much constant noise we were living with all the time as the Yanks moved about the streets, carting goods, barking orders. . . .

But the peace and quiet were suddenly shattered as the buggy drove down the long driveway leading to the plantation house. I heard a terrible commotion, and when we drew up to the front door I could see why—there was a huge throng of slaves near the far end of the main house, all of them crying and calling out, one or two screaming in the most horrible way. Mary's man hurried me out of the buggy, up the steps to the front porch, and into the house, away from the disturbance. He led me to a small back parlor with large windows that looked out onto the grounds. Mary was sitting in a high-backed chair, working on her needlepoint, and a tea service was already set out on a small table.

"Hello, Hannah," she said, smiling. "I am so pleased you could come."

I wanted desperately to ask what was transpiring outside, but I dared not. It would have been impolite to ask about something that was happening in another's home. I could only hope Mary would tell me.

"I simply couldn't sit here alone another minute," Mary exclaimed once I was seated. "Are you not completely overwrought about tonight?"

"I am," I responded. "Why, I barely closed my eyes all night! Do you really think our boys will come tomorrow?"

"I think they want revenge bad for the battles we lost at Corinth and Iuka." She paused. "Have you heard from Leon?"

I shook my head.

"I suspect he's a prisoner," Mary commiserated. "If he had died, you'd know. Or he could have been captured *and* be ill. Perhaps too ill to write . . ."

I hated being reminded of Leon and how he might be suffering. Why was Mary talking on and on about him? And although we had heard from Simon recently, everyone knew that meant little. Each boy was a musket blast away from death at any time. One of my brothers could be gone already, without our family even knowing as of yet. Alone at night I would weep for them or, even worse, lie in a state of cold dread, chilled to the bone under my blankets.

Mary had tears in her eyes. Suddenly I realized what the problem was.

"Mary Clark! You are soft on my Leon. Why on earth did you never say?"

"You know why, Hannah. Leon is too lively for me. He knows no fear. And I tremble at the least little thing. I am sure he thinks I am a terrible coward."

"Mary, you are a lady!" I admonished her. "You are not supposed to *exhibit* bravery of any sort! And you have such a lovely disposition. And you're so pretty! I'll wager my Leon never thought he had a hope. I have a suggestion. You write him a nice letter. And when we find out where he is, I'll send it. Just a friendly letter, no more, of course."

"Of course," Mary agreed. But her eyes sparkled now with the hope of the idea. "If only," she murmured, "he is still well."

Just then her twin brother, Robert, burst into the room. I felt a little heat rise up the back of my neck. I had liked Robert ever since I could remember. He had the same good looks as his sister, although his temperament was quite different from Mary's—he was hotheaded and quick to anger, while she was always serene. But I liked his passionate nature. In fact, he reminded me of Leon. It occurred to me that perhaps that was why Mary was secretly fond of Leon—she had grown up with someone of a similar character.

"That damned Ulysses Grant!" Robert exclaimed. "Why, he's created a madhouse here. A madhouse."

Mary leaped up to reprimand her brother. "Robert, we have a guest! Please apologize for cursing."

Robert offered me a short bow. "Miss Hannah, you won't scold me for cussing when you hear what's happened."

"What is it, Robert?" I asked, feeling the heat rise to my cheeks with the implied compliment.

"Robert!" Mary reprimanded him. "Hannah needn't hear this!"

Robert ignored her. "That General Grant has issued an order. They are building a contraband camp in Corinth, encouraging our slaves to run off! And at the very place of our defeat and our loss of so many boys! And now six of our slaves have tried to escape there! Six! We caught two and they are being punished. Twenty lashes."

"Twenty?" I gasped. "Will they live?"

"I don't know," Robert said gravely, "but they must be made an example. If not, that Lincoln will soon make sure we have no property left."

"That's enough of that kind of talk," Mary ordered her brother. "You know young ladies don't want to think about such things, Robert. Do we, Hannah?"

I shook my head. I did not. What if one of *our* slaves ran off? How would we manage? Why, Moses had practically taken over the running of the store. If he left, we simply would not be able to continue. It seemed the whole world was falling apart.

I must have said that aloud because Mary agreed with me.

"It is, Hannah. But we must be strong. Now, let us drink our tea and then do our needlework."

Robert cleared his throat and scuffed his boot against the carpet. "Will you put me down in your dance card, Miss Hannah?" he asked.

I was so thrilled, it was all I could do not to show my emotion. I paused for a moment to gather myself, then said, "We are serving punch, not dancing. However, we may be allowed one or two dances, and since you are the twin of my dear friend Mary, I *will* put you in my card."

"Well, that's fine, then," Robert said, and his face turned red and he stumbled a bit as he quickly left the room.

Mary gave me an amused look, but had the good manners not to embarrass me by teasing me about her brother. We sat quietly for a few moments, and I picked up some sewing to do out of the basket on the floor. Mary broke the silence, saying, "I wonder who they caught. I don't know any of the field hands personally that ran off, but Thom, one of our footmen, also ran, and I'd hate to see him hurt. Of course," she added quickly, "I know he needs to be punished, but I don't have to like it."

"I'm sure I won't like spanking my children when they misbehave," I said in an attempt at consoling her, "but I suppose I will have to do it."

"This is not a spanking," Mary said sharply.

I was shocked. Mary seemed to be sympathizing with them.

"There can be no room in your heart for such soft feelings," I scolded her. "This is war! And Lincoln will use those runaways against us. They could shoot and kill our brothers. Henry always says to me, 'We know this war is about states' rights. We know this war is about our being able to decide matters for ourselves. But the slaves don't know that! They believe all this Union talk that we're fighting over *them*! And that's a danger to us.'"

Mary looked up from her work and gazed at me. "You are right, Hannah, of course you are. I was being silly. Why don't we discuss literature? That is a safer topic, wouldn't you agree?"

I did agree. I was relieved as well. Such talk made me uncomfortable. It seemed the war was putting crazy ideas in everyone's head—even Mary's!

The time did go far quicker, however, than if I'd been at home or at the store. We had a lovely tea and discussed Miss Austen and Mr. Dickens. I rose to take my leave later in the afternoon. When I left the house there was no sign anything had happened. The slaves were all back at work. I couldn't help but remember the desperate screams I had heard on the way in, but I reminded myself that I must harden my heart.

When I got home it was time to get ready for the ball. I put on the dress of Joanna's I'd been working on and was pleased that it looked quite modern. Ma wore a soft gray satin gown, and Joanna wore a dress of white tulle with twisted green velvet bows. She looked stunning. I was only sorry all the Southern boys wouldn't get to see her, just the Northern louts. There were still boys my age left in town though, such as Mary's brother Robert. Secretly I had always imagined Joanna married to Mary's older brother, me married to Robert, and all of us living together on the plantation.

Before leaving, Ma gathered us in the dining room to light the Sabbath candles. She sang the prayer, and for a brief moment my nerves felt calmed as I listened to the beautiful melody and remembered a time when the entire family was together for Sabbath dinner. Ma also lit the silver menorah—three candles for the third night of Chanukah. Then she blew all the candles out. "It's wartime," she said, "and I'm sure God will understand that we have a shortage of candles."

I was just glad that Ma and Pa did not strictly observe the Sabbath or we might not be allowed to go to a dance on a Friday night.

As we arrived in our landau, carriages were pulling up one after another, and the scent of fresh flowers and food wafted out the open front door of the Hunter home. Mr. and Mrs. Hunter greeted their guests under the huge white columns of the front entrance. I noted that many of the guests were Federal officers. My stomach was simply a mass of butterflies. I could hardly stay calm enough to stop myself from trembling.

"You aren't catching a chill, are you, dear?" Ma asked as I shivered violently, stepping out of the landau.

"No, Ma, I am fine," I assured her. "I'm excited, that's all."

"Of course you are, dear," Ma said. "I wish your pa could see how beautiful you girls look. And how handsome you are, Henry dear."

Henry *was* looking rather fine, I thought. His black hair waved off his high brow, and his blue eyes were alight with excitement.

"And who will you be asking to dance tonight?" I teased him.

"Mellissa Horner, for one," he whispered to me. She was a year older than I was so I did not know her well, but she was pretty and seemed like an even-tempered young lady.

"Good luck," I whispered back.

We greeted the Hunters, and Mrs. Hunter shook my hand with especial warmth. I hurried to the ballroom. The three other girls were already behind the punch table serving—Eugenia and Mary looking beautiful, Claudia as plain as ever. They exchanged conspiratorial looks with me.

Eugenia pointed out three smaller bowls of punch at

the end of the table. "Those are for us," she explained. "No liquor. And of course for the rest of the girls. We don't want them getting liquored up and drunk."

I had to smile at the thought of all those proper young ladies with too much drink in them. The orchestra was already playing the waltz, and the officers, the older men still left in town, and the young boys were dancing with the beautifully dressed women. It all looked so gay. It almost seemed normal, if you could be blind to the color of the uniforms, that is. And if you didn't notice the orchestra playing "The Jefferson Davis Waltz" and "The Girl I Left Behind Me," songs that had become favorites because of the war.

Joanna and Captain Mazer glided across the floor, looking as if their feet were barely touching its gleaming surface. I had to admit that they cut a fine figure, but I was disgusted with her for flaunting their friendship so openly. I tried to ignore them and to concentrate on my duties.

We made sure to keep the drinks flowing, and soon the soldiers were having a wonderful time. After a couple of hours I desperately wanted to join those on the dance floor and was thrilled when Robert presented himself.

"I have come to claim my dance," he said with a small bow. I almost giggled, he looked so dignified.

The dance was a waltz, and he spun me around the room until I became dizzy, but I would never have asked him to stop. He held me lightly yet firmly in his arms, and he smiled down at me with a confidence I didn't know he possessed. When he returned me to the table, my cheeks must have been glowing with pleasure. It had been quite perfect, everything I'd dreamed it would be.

Robert also seemed flushed with the moment, because at the first break in the music he began to sing "The Bonnie Blue Flag" at the top of his lungs. Soon all the other young boys had joined in.

> *"We are a band of brothers, and native to the soil,*
> *Fighting for the property we gained by honest toil;*
> *And when our rights were threatened, the cry rose near and far:*
> *'Hurrah for the Bonnie Blue Flag that bears a single star!'*
> *Hurrah! Hurrah!*
> *For Southern rights, Hurrah!*
> *Hurrah for the Bonnie Blue Flag that bears a single star."*

The Yanks seemed not to know what to do, so they chose to ignore the singing. Or perhaps they were too drunk to care.

Right after the singing finished, Eugenia called all of us girls around her.

"Hannah," she whispered, "Ma just told me that old Mr. Perry saw Mrs. Grant and her son taking a carriage to the train station. They are leaving! But look at the soldiers. They don't seem to know what she must know."

"I don't understand," Mary said. "Why aren't the soldiers being called away from the party? Why aren't they getting ready? General Grant must know our boys are coming."

"Perhaps," I laughed, "he forgot to tell anyone but her!"

"Or maybe he told them, all right," Claudia said with a smile, "and no one believed it. Well, won't they be sorry!"

I couldn't stop from laughing and smiling the rest of the night. The Yanks would be sorry. And soon!

December 20, 1862

"Hannah, Hannah, wake up! The cavalry is here! Wake up!"

I stared at Joanna, who was shaking me by the shoulders as if I were a sack of potatoes. For a few seconds I had no idea what she was talking about or what was happening. I sat bolt upright in bed when her words finally began to make sense.

"Our boys?" I asked.

It was Henry who answered as he ran into my room. "Our boys are here! Our boys are here!"

"It's happening," I said to myself. "It's really happening!" I exclaimed to Joanna and Henry.

I threw on my dressing gown and ran out into the hallway, followed by Joanna and Henry. Ma was already on the landing, wrapped in her dressing gown, and David staggered out of his room, rubbing his eyes. We raced down the stairs with nary a thought about ladylike behavior, and Ma threw open the doors of the house. Dawn was just breaking and the sky was a pale blue with streaks of orange. Riding right past our house was a Confederate cavalry division. The street was already filled with women and children who were cheering, "Hurrah for Jefferson Davis," and waving Confederate flags.

Those soldiers seemed to me to be the finest sight I had ever seen. I added my voice to the others, cheering as loudly as I could. At the same time I listened expectantly for the sound of gunfire but heard nothing at all.

"The Yanks have all been caught sleeping, I bet!" I shouted above the noise of the horses and the cheering. "They don't seem to be putting up a fight."

"What do you mean?" Joanna cried.

"I mean we got them so drunk last night they couldn't aim a gun if their life depended on it!" I was jumping up and down in joy and triumph.

Joanna grabbed me by both shoulders. "Do you mean to say you knew this was to happen?"

The look in her eyes alarmed me and I was suddenly afraid to say anything.

"Answer me!" Joanna shook me hard.

"Yes!" I said defiantly. "I knew! And I helped!"

Joanna let go of me. She stared at me for a moment, then slapped me across the cheek with all the force she could muster.

I reeled away, stunned. I staggered and would have fallen into the path of a horse that was charging by had Henry not caught hold of me.

Joanna turned around and ran up the steps of the house, tears flowing down her face.

"You knew?" Henry asked.

I clutched my cheek and nodded. "I couldn't tell," I muttered. "I'd sworn!"

"Then you did right," Henry said. "An oath is sacred. I wondered why Mrs. Hunter was being so generous with her liquor, it being in such short supply these days—and to waste it on those Yanks . . . I couldn't understand it." He grinned. "Good for you, little sister. Pa is always telling me never to underestimate the womenfolk."

Fortunately Ma had missed the entire episode with Joanna. She was too busy watching David, making sure that he didn't get into trouble. Holding on to him tightly, she hurried over to Henry and me.

"Hannah!" she exclaimed. "What happened to your face?"

I wasn't sure what to tell her. I was torn. I wanted Ma to know how horrid Joanna had been to me, but I also knew that tattling was not the behavior of a lady. It wasn't honorable.

Henry saved me. "She tripped," he said quickly.

"Silly girl," Ma scolded. "You'll need a cold compress on that or it will swell right up."

I nodded. "In a minute, Ma. I just want to be out here for now." A little voice inside began to worry. Although I *knew* I'd done the right thing, if Ma found out, perhaps she wouldn't agree. Ma liked Captain Mazer, after all. I could only hope that Joanna wouldn't say anything about my part in all of this.

A soldier doffed his cap to Ma and me and offered a little bow as he rode by. I could see others doing the same to our neighbors. They seemed genuinely moved by the welcome they were receiving—women with their hair loose, still in their nightdresses or robes, children in their nightclothes, old men hobbling out into the patios, all in an ecstasy of delight at their arrival. And even better, we began to see a few Federals who had no guns, and weren't even dressed! They were wandering, completely baffled, out onto the streets in their underclothes!

"You children are going to catch your death out here," Ma finally declared. "You can watch from the window," she said. "Everyone get dressed, and I'll have Emily cook a nice, hot breakfast. Go on, now."

Henry and David and I raced one another upstairs to our rooms to dress, each of us calling on Jule for help. Once dressed in my dark blue cloth, which was warm in case I wanted to be outdoors more during the day, I hurried down to the breakfast room. Ma seemed to take forever dressing, and Joanna came to the table, eyes red with weeping. Emily, our cook, served us grits, and as we ate, Ma spoke to us in a rather stern voice.

"Children, you must not get underfoot of the soldiers. Accidents can happen. I want all of you to stay close to home. Henry and I will open the store, the rest of you will stay here."

"Ma," complained Henry, "why open the store? No one will buy today! Our boys have all they need from Union supplies, and the townsfolk will be too busy cheering to feel like shopping!"

Ma considered for a moment. "You may be right, dear. But your pa has had that store open every day since we built it, and I don't want to be the one to tell him we left it closed—even for a day."

Henry obviously could think of no good argument in return, so he shrugged and said, "Fine, Ma, we'll go if you are so stuck on it." And they rose from the table in order to get ready.

That was when I heard and felt the first explosion.

"What was that?" David squealed. "Did something

go *kaboom*?" Something had gone *kaboom*, but what?

We all ran to the window, but we couldn't see where the sound had come from, so we rushed to the door. The first thing we saw when Henry opened the door was a huge plume of smoke rising in the air from the central depot, where the engine house, the station house, and the storehouses were located.

Henry understood immediately what was happening. "The Federal supplies," he said, "they are going to burn them all!"

"But the town—that will set fire to the whole town!" I protested. That made no sense to me. After all, we were talking about our own boys!

"What did you think they were going to do with the supplies?" Joanna snapped at me. "*Confiscate* them? Ask the Federals please not to use them again?"

"Why can't they keep them?" David asked.

"Because they aren't staying," Henry concluded. "If they were staying, they *would* keep them. They can't stand up to all the Federal troops around here. Soon they'd be surrounded. They'll burn it all and get out. That's my guess."

"But maybe there are other Confederate troops behind them," I said. "This is just the beginning! It must be!" I couldn't accept what Henry was saying. Would we be right back in Yankee hands?

"Henry must be right," Ma said, shaking her head. "If they were planning on staying, they wouldn't burn those storehouses. They'd keep all this for our boys. If they can't stay, they don't want the Union boys to have any of it."

Another explosion rocked the house, this one closer.

"Henry," Ma said, "you go out and see what's happening. We'll wait here."

We waited for Henry in the front parlor, barely speaking. I was in a fit of different emotions. Just to see our boys so close was glorious, but to know they would be leaving was almost unbearable. Even more unbearable was the possibility that they might destroy parts of our town. And, naturally, I had hoped that Simon or Leon would be with these troops, but we certainly would have heard from them by now were that the case. So that was terribly disappointing. And then that little voice kept nagging at me about Joanna. Had I betrayed my own sister in some way? She sat quietly, wringing her handkerchief in her hands, dabbing at the tears in her eyes, a picture of misery.

There was a knock at the door, and Jule showed in Mrs. Potter from next door.

"I came to inquire," she said, "if you might know what those explosions were." She had snow-white hair and settled herself slowly into a chair at Ma's invitation.

"We've sent Henry off to find out," Ma assured her.

Only moments later Mr. Gray from three doors down was shown in with the same question. He, too, sat down. Then Kate Freemont, a girl of ten who lived on our other side, rushed into the room.

"Granddad says they captured all fifteen hundred soldiers," she announced, "and then paroled them all! What's the use of that, letting them go?"

"They've paroled all of them?" Joanna asked. "There was no fighting?"

"Actually, Pa says the Second Illinois Cavalry set up defenses at the fairground. They were fighting hand to hand, with their swords! But they were defeated by the First Mississippi Cavalry and taken prisoner. They were no match for our boys. Of course not! They took quite a beating, I heard."

"Any dead?" Joanna asked, her voice faint.

"Some, Pa says. And lots more wounded."

Joanna let out a strangled cry.

Henry burst into the room then. "You know all the flour outside the depot—must've been a half mile of barrels, at least fifteen feet high? They threw turpentine over it and they've burned it all! That's where all the smoke is coming from. Plus the hundreds of bales of cotton? They're burning them, too!

"I spoke to one of our lads. He couldn't believe how beautiful it is here, how it doesn't even look like there's been a war. He said it was too bad that after the Federals left it all nice, it had to be them, our own boys, who'd have to ruin our town! But it has to be done, he said. Then he told me that they were going to fire up all the buildings that are stuffed with supplies—the town square, the courthouse, the livery building, post office, everything! He assured me when I became concerned over our store that they would try to spare anything that served the townsfolk, not the Federals."

A loud knock at the door made us all gasp, we had been listening so intently to Henry. As for me, I did not want to believe what I was hearing. But I would soon learn it was all too true. Jule announced a Lieutenant

Dean, who was a small man with a very large mustache. Ma rose to greet him. "Lieutenant?"

"Ma'am. I'm sorry to inform you, ma'am, that you and your family must leave this house. We are evacuating all homes along here. The buildings hereabouts are filled with armaments, and when we blow them—well, we can't guarantee your safety. My apologies, ma'am. Please excuse me. I must go to the next house." And he left.

We just stared at one another. For a moment we could not move or speak. *It can't be so,* I kept thinking to myself over and over. *They wouldn't. They couldn't.* Mrs. Potter, Mr. Gray, and Kate all took their leave so they could join their own families.

Ma seemed stuck to the floor in one spot and couldn't seem to take any action. Moses appeared at the door. "Missus," he said, "I told Jule and Emily to pack bags for the family. They's doin' it now. Maybe the young'uns should go and help 'em."

"Yes, yes of course, Moses. Thank you," Ma said. "But where should we go?"

"Away from the square, that's for sure. You want to send a note to someone?"

"Perhaps the Hunters," Ma said slowly. "Pa is a particular friend to Mr. Hunter, and you and Eugenia are so close." She looked at me to see if I approved, but I could be of no help since I had not yet accepted that we should really have to go. She moved to the desk, where she seated herself with a pen and paper. As she dipped the quill into the inkwell she seemed to me not so much calm as stunned.

"The children should pack what's dear to 'em," Moses said gently. "And in a hurry, missus."

"Moses," I said weakly, "we don't really have to pack, do we? They could never destroy our home. Never."

Moses shook his head with sympathy. "Miss Hannah," he said, "this may be your only chance to save what you hold dear. Now, you get yourself goin'. Mebbe it won't happen. But if it does, an' you didn't take your favorite things, why, I guess you'd be pretty sad."

Slowly, almost as if it were a dream, I followed Henry and David up the stairs. I could hear Joanna calling after us, "Whatever Emily packs is fine for me, Moses. I don't care."

But I cared. I gazed around my precious room: the four-poster bed draped with a soft yellow muslin; the wardrobe, already being emptied by Jule; the shelves with my doll collection; and my miniature dollhouse laid out on a small, intricately carved wooden table. It was the dollhouse I wanted to take most of all, but it would never fit in my trunk.

Quickly my eyes scanned my shelves and I surveyed my dolls. I chose three favorites—the porcelain child, the Pierrot, and the clown—and felt like I was abandoning the rest. I picked up my diary and looked at it. I'd had no time to write in it over the last few days. I would need to catch up. I placed it in the trunk along with three small statuettes I took off my shelves—a horse, a dog, and an adorable circus bear Pa had brought all the way from the old country. I took the mother-of-pearl hand mirror and the matching comb and brush set Ma and Pa had given me for my twelfth birthday off my dresser and packed them. I chose the darling music box they had given me on my eleventh birthday, and I put all my jewelry in the intricately carved rosewood jewel box that had once belonged to Great-Grandmother.

What else? What else? I looked around frantically, then started to help Jule with the clothes.

"Maybe the house won't be damaged, Jule," I said as I helped her fold my dresses. "Maybe they feel it is simply better to be safe than sorry."

"Which of these dresses, missy?" Jule asked.

I chose as best I could, then turned my attention to my books. Pa had helped me build a large collection, and my books seemed to me to be as good friends as my friends of flesh and blood. I sat down on my bed in despair. How could I choose?

"You best get a move on, missy," Jule said. "I don't want to be near here when they start blowin' things up!"

"They won't, Jule, they won't!" I said fiercely. "It's our boys." Then I repeated again to myself, "Our boys."

"Well, just in case," Jule said, unmoved, "you hurry yourself."

I looked at my shelves and chose my Jane Austen collection and my brand-new book by Charles Dickens, *David Copperfield*. I included the books of Rebekah Hyneman, poetry about women in the Bible. My favorite poem was "Deborah." She was a warrior. A real warrior. I wished at that moment that I, too, could be one, because then I could do *something*. And I would save our house. I would.

I sat down at my desk. My eyes fell immediately on *The Catechism for Jewish Children*. It was Pa who had always taught us our lessons, both in reading Hebrew and in studying about Judaism, but since the war began, Ma had let it all slip. I felt a pang of regret. I had enjoyed the lessons with Pa, who had had Uncle Jacob send a copy of the *Catechism,* written by Rabbi Isaac Leeser, from Philadelphia. I opened the booklet and my eyes fell on one of the first questions posed:

> What is meant by Conscience?
> It is that sensation which tells us (if we have been correctly instructed) whether we have done right or wrong; and if our conduct has been correct, it makes us feel satisfied; but if we have done wrong, it makes us ashamed and dissatisfied with ourselves.

Again that little voice appeared and gave me just such an uncomfortable feeling. Was that voice telling me I had done wrong by Joanna? But it was for the South! Wasn't that more important even than family? Especially if the family was on the wrong path, like Joanna was? And yet, if I had spoken up and the Federals had been ready, maybe our house would not be on the verge of being destroyed.

I tossed the booklet into the trunk along with my other things and tried to stop thinking.

Ma stepped into the room.

"The Hunters will have us," she said. "Finish packing. We have very little time."

I could see Ma's eyes were red. "Joanna has gone out," Ma added. "I think she's gone to see if she can find Captain Mazer. When you are finished here, Hannah, go to her room and help Emily."

"Yes, Ma," I said. What could Joanna be thinking? What could she do? The captain was either captured, dead, or paroled. If paroled, he would find Joanna. How would she ever find him? I felt a little queasy. If the captain were dead? Well, I told myself, those thoughts I had been having just moments earlier were weak and foolish. This was war. Captain Mazer's fate had nothing to do with me. My conscience was clear.

"Don't just stand there, Hannah," Ma said sharply. "Hurry!"

, , ,

As we got into the carriage another explosion from the direction of the train station shook the town. Soldiers swarmed in the streets, most of them smoking cigars, obviously taken from the storehouses. Many of them had three or four pistols sticking out of their coat jacket and almost all of them were swigging whisky straight from the bottle. They all seemed to be rushing somewhere. A few hundred yards away I noticed a rakish-looking man on a black mare.

"That's General Van Dorn!" Henry exclaimed.

"The one who lost the battle of Corinth?" Ma asked.

"Yes," Henry said. "The very one. But he hasn't lost this battle."

"There was no battle!" I snapped. "Only a whole bunch of men too drunk to put up a fight."

Henry gave me a puzzled look as we settled into our seats. "These are our boys, Hannah," he reminded me, as if I had not been repeating that to myself over and over again.

"Who are about to destroy our house," I replied. And then, as we drove away, I felt quite overcome by emotions, terrified and angry at the same time. And I was so confused—I had pictured this as a perfect day. How could it have turned out so wrong? Everything in my life had always been perfectly orderly. It felt now as if it had suddenly turned to pure confusion and disorder. Would I ever see my dear home again? How would Pa feel when he returned, longing for home the way he must be, only to find that there was no home left?

"I hope they'll not take both," Ma said.

"Both?" I asked.

"The store. It is on the other side of the square. We may be left with neither."

I was feeling more and more panic-stricken every moment.

"What's that smell?" David exclaimed.

The most nauseating odor began to fill up the carriage as we drove along, and the smoke was so thick it was becoming hard to see anything outside of the carriage with any clarity. And I wanted to see everything. I wanted to fix in my mind these beautiful homes, these stately streets lined with trees and decorated with flower beds. My memory of them might soon be all that was left.

"The soldiers I spoke to told me those railroad carriages were filled to the brim with all kinds of food—especially bacon," Henry said, explaining the overpowering odor.

I put my handkerchief over my mouth and nose and tried very hard not to be sick. Another explosion, then another, came from that area, and the sky filled with a thick, acrid smoke.

"Where is Joanna?" Ma fretted. "She isn't safe out in this. She knew we were going to the Hunters'. I only hope she has the sense to meet us there!"

Another, even larger explosion rocked the carriage, and suddenly the horses bolted. I could hear Moses yelling at them, "Whoa there!" as the carriage careened from one side to the other and we all fell one on top of the other. David screamed, "Ma, Ma," and Henry swore, "What the devil is wrong with that boy, he'll get us killed!" I was too frightened to say anything at all and was sure we were about to meet our doom when the carriage came to an abrupt halt. A young soldier, one of ours, opened the door as we were righting ourselves.

"You all right in here?" he asked. "I managed to get ahold of your horse there and calm him down. Nasty bit of noise, no wonder he took bad."

"Thank you, sir," Ma said, her voice shaking. "You have saved my family and me from certain injury."

"Well, it's my pleasure, ma'am," he replied, and he closed the door. Moses called down to see if we were unhurt, and when Ma assured him we were, we continued on our way.

One by one we all began to cough from the smoke. I could barely breathe. Moses dropped us at the Hunters' front door and turned the carriage right around to go back for our trunks. Once indoors we breathed a little easier, as the Hunters had shut all the doors and windows up tight. Eugenia took my hand and led me into the front parlor. "This is unspeakable," she said. "Not your house!"

I was so shaken from the carriage ride that I barely heard her. For the moment I was just happy to be alive. Mrs. Hunter brought the rest of the family into the front parlor, sat us down, and made sure we drank some hot tea. And then a terrifying explosion rattled the entire house.

"That must have been the town square," Mrs. Hunter said.

Eugenia took my hand. "Maybe your house survived," she said. "We can pray."

, ,

Explosion after explosion shook the very foundation of the Hunters' home, and we sat in the parlor, unable even to think of any small thing to say. I felt quite numb, as if it were all some cruel dream from which I was bound to wake. After we had been there half an hour or so, Joanna staggered into the room. She was covered in soot so dark that her green dress appeared black. Her face, too, was black and grimy, her hair falling about her, disheveled and wild.

Ma ran to her and grasped Joanna's trembling hands. "Oh, my dear. Are you all right? What has happened? What is your news?"

Joanna sank to the floor. Henry rushed over to her, as did Eugenia, and they helped her up and then into a chair.

Mrs. Hunter instructed Eugenia to run and get Poppie to heat water for a tub. Then we all waited for Joanna to speak. I was holding my breath, afraid, I suppose, of what she might say.

She began to weep. "I couldn't see him," she managed to get out. "He'd been sorely injured, and the doctor was trying to sew up his wounds. I spoke to Private Katz, who escaped unhurt. Jonathan leaped in front of a sword slash that would surely have killed his friend. In doing so he saved his friend's life and possibly forfeited his own." She wept harder. "That's the kind of person he is. Always thinking of others." She glared hard at me. "Unlike some people I could mention."

I desperately wanted to answer back. I *had* been thinking of others. The Confederate boys! But I bit my tongue. I knew that the Hunters were on my side in this matter and that I needn't defend myself.

Eugenia returned to say that they could take Joanna to one of the guest rooms to get cleaned up. Then she bit her lip and looked as though she were searching for words.

"I'm afraid I have some bad news," she said softly. She looked sadly at me. "Moses tells me that the explosion has completely destroyed your home. There is little left but rubble. He was able to take away all your luggage, though," she added.

At this news Ma fell into a faint, and Mrs. Hunter had to administer smelling salts. I sat where I was, frozen, unable to think or speak or move.

Joanna was taken away to bathe. I was led to Eugenia's room and put to bed with a cold compress on my cheek, which was now quite red and swollen from Joanna's earlier slap. My head was swimming and I felt ill. Everything gone? All the beautiful things Ma and Pa had bought over the years. The dishes brought all the way from Germany. Portraits of the family and of their grandparents in the old country. My perfect little room. All my books and toys. The safety of our own home. Where would we live now? What would become of us?

The house trembled under the force of another explosion. I began to scream. I screamed until my screams turned to sobs. Henry ran in and held my hand and tried to soothe me. Eugenia tried as well. But I could not be consoled.

December 21, 1862

When I awoke in Eugenia's bed, I thought the previous day must have been a bad dream. Fire, smoke, and destruction, that's all I could remember—that and my sister's hatred. I lay in bed, eyes open, and didn't have the strength to sit up. Eugenia was fast asleep beside me. Well, she *could* sleep. She still had her home. What would my family do? And where was Pa? Ma had written him four times a day. Still, with all this trouble who knew if he had even received her letters.

A soft knock at the door woke Eugenia. It was her personal servant, Lucy.

"Miss Eugenia, Miss Hannah. Miss Hannah's ma, she got some letters just now. She wants Miss Hannah. She's in the back guest room. I'll show Miss Hannah the way."

I began to tremble. Letters. Was one of them from a commanding officer telling our family of Simon's or Leon's death? "Please, God," I whispered, "please, God." I muttered my prayers as I walked, all the way down the long hallway toward the room Ma was staying in. The rest of the family was there already, gathered around the bed. Ma sat propped up by pillows, hair loose around her shoulders, skin pale, almost sallow. She looked as if she had aged a hundred years. Once I arrived, she spoke.

"I have two letters," she said. "One from the War Department, one from Simon. The postmaster brought the one from the War Department. Simon managed to get a fellow going to Oxford on leave to bring this.

When he saw the house had been destroyed, he asked around until he was told where we were, bless him." She took a deep breath. "I'll open the one from the War Department first," she said, her voice shaking. She opened it and began to read:

> "Dear Mrs. Green,
>
> "I regret to inform you that your son Leon was taken prisoner after a battle near Corinth. We will endeavor to have him exchanged as part of a prisoner-of-war trade but can, as of now, only hope for the best. He distinguished himself admirably despite being unwell the day of the fight.
>
> "I am sorry to send you this news. We pray for his speedy recovery and his release.
>
> > "Captain C. Everette"

"My poor, dear child," Ma whispered. She looked at the date. "It is dated October. The postmaster said it was sent then and somehow went astray."

Henry spoke up first. "At least he's alive, Ma," he said.

I pictured the last time I'd seen Leon—his thick black hair going every which way, untamable as always, the sparkle in his eyes, his mischievous wink to me as he departed. Leon always had a joke for me; he was always the one to cheer everyone else up. And I didn't doubt, even in his adversity, that he would continue to do the same. *If only he could be home,* I thought, *so we could nurse him!* The thought of him being ill, being a prisoner in some horrible camp, with no Ma or sisters to care for him—

why, it was too much to bear. Ma sank back into the pillows, tears flowing down her cheeks. Joanna sat beside her on the bed, weeping too, trying to console her with soft words.

"I'll read Simon's letter," I offered. I opened it delicately, feeling I was holding something more precious than gold in my hand.

"'December sixteenth. My dearest family,'" I read, but then my throat seemed to close with emotion and I could read no further. I beheld Simon so clearly as soon as I viewed his handwriting—Simon, who was small, as was Ma, with light brown curly hair like Ma's too. Simon, who was a true scholar. Pa was so proud of him. He would go to university if he survived the war and become a great expert on something—it seemed there was no subject he could not master.

Henry was forced to take the letter from me. He proceeded to read: "'We have recently been engaged in some of the fiercest fighting yet at Fredricksburg. The Federals have a new general called Burnside. I deem our side lucky to have no such fool in command! He tried to cross the Rappahannock River using pontoon bridges, but there was one problem: They had to build the bridges, and we kept shooting at them, which made that task mighty difficult. There was a thick fog, so I guess they assumed we wouldn't be able to find them, but well, we just aimed at the *noise* they were making, and I guess our aim was pretty fine! Finally they started to shell us with all the artillery they could muster, but we held our ground. We held them off for sixteen hours, and that allowed General Longstreet to fortify his positions. At one point we fought the Federals street by street—but were forced to leave the town to them. We withdrew behind a stone wall on a rise called Marye's Heights and joined the thousands of troops well installed there. The Federals sent their men in wave after wave, and even we, their enemies, had to admire their ferocity. They were cut down, though, with a terrible ease and it was nothing less than a slaughter. Thousands upon thousands died. Although the Yanks got hurt far worse than we did, we suffered too. And here I must prepare you for some heavy news.

"'George Clark, my dear friend, was severely wounded in the chest. With some help I took him to a cottage, where a friendly family agreed to let me nurse him. There I sat by his side, read to him from the Bible, and when it became obvious he was dying, I held him in my arms until he was gone.'"

"Oh, dear heavens," Ma murmured. "Not George."

I glanced at Joanna. She was biting her lip and shaking her head. As for me, the news slammed into me with the force of a horse's hoof.

Henry continued. "'There was, as always, confusion, and his name apparently did not make it onto the list of the dead. I have written his family with the sad news.

"'My dear Joanna, I must tell you that George spoke of little else but you those last hours. He had often asked me about your heart. I know you were fond of him, and a better husband I'm sure you could not have found. But God had other plans for George. Please take comfort in the fact that he died with a dear friend and companion with him, and that his suffering was mitigated by the tender care he received.

"I have been much comforted by a prayer sent to all the Jewish Confederate soldiers by the Reverend Michelbacher, who I am sure you remember is the rabbi of the Beth Ahabah congregation in Richmond. He has had enough printed out so that we Israelites may carry the prayer with us. Myself and the other Israelites in my company try to have a small service on the Sabbath if it is at all possible.

"I quote you a few small portions of his prayer here in the hope that it might comfort you as it does me.

"'"This once happy country is inflamed by the fury of war; a menacing enemy is arrayed against the rights, liberties and freedom of this, our Confederacy; The ambition of this enemy has dissolved fraternal love. . . . Our firesides are threatened; the foe is before us, with the declared intention to desecrate our soil, to murder our people. O Lord, God of Israel, be with me in the hot season of the contending strife; protect and bless me with health and courage to bear cheerfully the hardships of war.

"'"O Lord, Ruler of Nations, destroy the power of our enemies! . . . O Almighty God of Israel, as thou didst strike for thy people on the plains of Canaan— guide them, O Lord of Battles, into the paths of victory, guard them from the shaft and missile of the enemy . . . and battle in thy name to win."'"

"Stop!" Joanna was on her feet, her face hot with fury.

Henry looked up, amazed. I had been so caught up in the prayer my heart jumped at the sound of Joanna's voice.

"This is unconscionable," Joanna cried.

"You are upset, dear," Ma said. "Please try to calm yourself."

"I will not! Why does that reverend believe that God is on the Confederate side? How can he say such things? How can he corrupt our boys with such a prayer? And the Union boys—has God turned away from *them*? Is that what we are to believe?"

I felt my ire rising. "George is dead," I cried, leaping up and glaring at Joanna. "Leon is a prisoner. Don't you even care?"

"Of course I care, Hannah. I cannot abide the thought of our poor dear Leon ill, a prisoner. . . . But my Jonathan is dreadfully sick too. Can't you see they are the same? How can you be so blind?"

"Joanna," I retorted, "it is you who are blind."

"You know everything, do you not?" Joanna declared. "You know that the South is right, the North is wrong."

I hardly felt like dignifying her with an answer. And I was so distressed about Leon and George I did not want to engage in an argument with her. But I felt I could not let her remark pass. I snapped back, "You knew that too, until you met Captain Mazer."

"That is true," Joanna said. "That is so true. Because until I met Captain Mazer and discovered what a good heart he has, I had looked at all their boys as evil and bad."

"All their boys *are* evil," Henry exclaimed. "They

want to rule us. They know no honor. They would murder us in our beds, given the chance."

"Jonathan wouldn't want to see so much as a fly get hurt," Joanna protested. "He certainly doesn't want us to be *murdered*! He is good and only wants good! And if he is good, then others like him, other Federals, might be good too. At least that is what I reasoned."

"Reason!" I snorted. "What you indulge in is the opposite of reason."

"Madness," Henry agreed. "You have gone mad!"

"I simply saw him for himself," Joanna said, glaring at Henry. "And once I did that, Jonathan and I were able to converse in earnest. And he encouraged me to look at the Negroes in the same way, as individuals."

I gasped. I could not believe she had uttered those words.

"Yes, you may gape like a fish, little sister. But has it ever occurred to you that our Negroes are human beings, much like we are?"

"No!" I cried. "It has not! Why, they are inferior to us in every way! Ma," I said, turning to her, "did you know that Captain Mazer was an abolitionist?"

Ma, still pale from all the terrible news, was too weak to reply. She shook her head.

"Well, I for certain didn't," Henry said. "If those Yanks don't murder us while we sleep, then they'd be just as happy getting our slaves to do it for them. That's what they are up to, you know. They encourage the slaves to kill their owners. Why, Joanna, you're not showing any good sense at all!"

"*I'm* showing a lack of good sense?" Joanna sputtered, her cheeks pink with anger. "Listen to that prayer you were reading, Henry. What kind of God would choose sides? God cares about one thing and one thing only. That we behave with charity and goodness. According to that rabbi, God has turned his back on Jonathan." She began to weep. "But I tell you He has not! He has him in His loving arms and He will take care of him just the way He will care for our boys."

"The devil will care for their boys," I declared.

"There is no devil!" Joanna shouted at me. "Don't you remember what Pa used to teach us? God loves all creatures. Go get your catechism, Hannah. You have filled your heart with hatred. You have filled your heart with hatred until it is a cold, cruel thing. You are sad now because your house is destroyed. You are not sad for the loss you see everywhere. You are not sad for the injuries we impose on one another."

I felt an anger so immense, so cold, wash over me that in that moment I could have killed Joanna and not felt a moment of regret.

"How *dare* you?" I said, my voice cracking with emotion. "You say I have no feeling? *I* will weep for George even if you will not! *I* will weep for Leon, lying in some camp, shot by Captain Mazer's compatriots, perhaps near death himself. *I* will—"

"Children!" Ma exclaimed, her voice raised almost to a shout. "None of you will say another word, and we will all pretend this conversation never happened. Hannah, go back to Eugenia's room and dress. We are going to the house to see if we can recover anything. Then we must go to the store and see if we can open. If we can, we must. We cannot afford to go a day without trade."

I looked at Ma in shock. She never raised her voice. I darted a quick look at Joanna. She was still glaring at me as if ready to strike me again. Well, I would listen to Ma and not give Joanna a chance. I didn't want to admit to myself that I had become a little frightened of Joanna. So I tossed my head, turned, and without another word walked out of the room.

I had the hard, unenviable task of retelling all the bad news to Eugenia. I also recounted the argument Joanna and I had had. Eugenia was dismayed.

"Why," Eugenia exclaimed, "it sounds as if she is being convinced by her captain that this war is about slaves, when we all know it is not. It is about our right here in Mississippi to decide for ourselves, to make our own rules. My pa has explained it all to me perfectly clearly. And without our slaves how does your dear sister think we could live? Who would do the work? I am afraid she is living in a dream world."

I agreed with Eugenia. How could Joanna have gone so far astray? And how could she accuse me of such horrible things? It was preposterous! It was ludicrous! It was . . . it was plain mean!

Still fuming over Joanna and grieving over Leon, I went down for breakfast. Once Mrs. Hunter had assured herself that our plates were well filled with food, she spoke. "I am so sorry to tell you," she said, "that the

Confederates have withdrawn from town, and we are once again under the control of the Union, specifically the paroled Federal troops."

"They are all gone?" I asked. "Already?"

"Yes, dear," she replied. "And I'm afraid they've left very little of the town square. The destruction is something terrible, I understand. They are saying, though, that this little raid might just have saved Vicksburg from the Union. Without these supplies General Grant can no longer feed his troops for the advance on Vicksburg he had planned. And so your sacrifice will be for something, at least," she said to Ma.

That is what I must remember, I told myself. *Our sacrifice may help us win the war. It may bring Simon and Leon home sooner.* And yet, in my heart, all I wanted was my home back and things as they had been before yesterday.

After breakfast, just before getting in the carriage, Ma spoke to Moses. "After you take us to the house, Moses, you may drive Miss Joanna around and let her ask some questions. Perhaps she can find out where the wounded are being tended. And make sure Jule and Emily meet us at the house."

"Yes, ma'am," Moses replied. "I have already sent them on ahead."

As I looked at Moses, Joanna's words flooded back to me. And it seemed so obvious to me that she had lost all sense and reason. Why, Moses' only reason for living was to help us. What would he do if he were free? He'd live in squalor somewhere, no doubt, and finally starve to death.

We drove toward where our house used to stand.

Although smoke still lingered in the air, all the houses along the way were untouched and it looked as if nothing had happened—until we reached the town square. When we arrived there, Joanna hugged Ma and thanked her, and then after we had descended from the carriage, she drove on with Moses.

I stood and stared at the destruction all around. The entire south half of the square had been leveled. Fires still smoldered in the ruins. Where once beautiful mansions had lined the street, now all that was left was rubble. Neighbors were sifting through the wreckage, and there was an eerie quiet as people spoke softly to one another, as if all the life and energy had gone right out of them.

Henry held Ma up on one side; David, trying to be a man, held her on the other. Jule and Emily were picking their way through the debris. Emily, who was a large woman with a short temper, spoke to Ma.

"There ain't much left, missus," she said, shaking her head. "I found this, though." She went back and brought out the silver menorah.

"Why," David exclaimed, "that's a miracle just like in the story! The Chanukah lamp has survived, Ma. That's a reminder to us from God, Ma. Miracles do happen!"

Ma knelt down by David and, tears flowing down her cheeks, she held him tight. "You are right, dear," she said. "We must remember God's miracles. And we must thank Him for what we have."

"And what is that?" I asked, feeling a distress so great I thought I might shatter into small pieces like a broken mirror.

"We have one another," Ma answered. "And although Leon is injured, he isn't dead. And we must pray for him."

I had never heard Ma talk of praying before. If Pa had been there though, he would have said that we decide, then God helps. I would have to talk to Pa about that. It seemed to me that I had been allowed to decide nothing. And if God was the one in control, I did not like His decisions. But praying for the boys certainly couldn't be a bad thing to do, and perhaps it would help. I resolved to pray whenever I could.

We left Jule and Emily to salvage what they could and walked over to the store. The south side had been spared because none of the buildings had contained Federal goods, and fortunately the fires had not spread. It was odd to see these few buildings intact: our store, the doctor's house, the Barneses' home, and the small hotel. The front of our store was a little blackened, but inside everything was just the way it had been left.

"People will need supplies today," Ma said. "We must get ready."

I didn't resent the work that morning. It took my mind off the image of our house, our dear house. I felt that if I began to cry now, I would simply never stop. Also it kept me too busy to think about Joanna and the awful things she had said. And, naturally, I assumed that the worst that could happen had happened.

How far from the truth that proved to be.

December 22, 1862

I walked slowly into the store the next morning, blessedly too tired to feel anything else but pure exhaustion. I had been run off my feet the day before. Everyone, it seemed, had needed something from our store. Oil lamps and lanterns were in high demand, many of them having been shattered by the blasts. Medicines, especially those for nerves, seemed to be the next most important item. After that, people wanted inkwells and quills—there would be many letters written about the raid to husbands and sons away. And for neighbors who had taken in neighbors there was all the extra food that was now necessary.

Mr. Hunter had told us at breakfast that General Grant was due to return to town. As one of the town's leaders, Mr. Hunter had been informed that since the Federals' stores had been destroyed, Grant had issued an order for his troops to take what they needed within a fifteen-mile radius around Holly Springs. And that meant from the townsfolk, the farmers, and the plantation owners. Goods would be confiscated. Mr. Hunter advised Mrs. Hunter to hide all their valuables.

The life of plenty that we had enjoyed up until that day was soon to be over, and we would surely feel the war as other towns had. I felt a deep sense of unease. I hadn't liked seeing my town occupied by the Yanks. In fact, I'd hated it. But, to their credit, they had behaved for the most part fairly decently. I wasn't sure, however, that that behavior would continue. They were bound to be angry—angry at being caught sleeping when the Confederates surprised them; angry at the womenfolk who had plied them with drink; angry at themselves for being made such fools. Everyone who had come into the store yesterday was worried that the Yanks would turn nasty. I wondered what form the nastiness would take. Would they ransack the town, taking what they pleased? Would they begin arresting the town leaders? Rather than feeling safe and secure at Eugenia's, I felt quite the opposite. Any minute I expected to hear soldiers knocking at the door. It was dreadful to feel so helpless.

I hadn't seen Joanna at all since she went off looking for Captain Mazer the day before. According to Ma, Joanna had found him in a building near the fairgrounds that the Federals were using as a field hospital. Joanna had come home late and left early. Apparently her news was that the captain would probably live. He had lost plenty of blood, but if the wound didn't become infected, there would be no lasting damage. They planned to send him home to Cincinnati as soon as he was strong enough. Joanna was talking to Ma about going with him so she could nurse him along the way.

I felt terrible about the rift that had developed between my sister and me. I didn't understand how it had happened so quickly. We had always been close, being the only two girls. We used to go to the dressmaker together and talk about young men and marriage. Joanna had taught me how to do needlepoint and had helped me with my music lessons. And when Joanna was away at finishing school in New Orleans, it was me she would write to about the pranks the girls played. Once Joanna had sewn a particularly nasty bully into her bed while the girl was sleeping. Then she and her friends woke the girl in the dead of night and made ghostly noises— groans and moans and unearthly cries. The girl begged to be loosed from her bonds, but Joanna would not let her go until she promised never to torment others again.

I laughed when I read that letter. It was so like Joanna, high-spirited and yet always concerned for others. I had always looked up to her. But now she was impossible to talk to and wouldn't listen to reason. She could only lecture and pass judgment on me, when it was she who was so obviously in the wrong! And to have fallen in love with an abolitionist! Why, it made my skin crawl. What I could not understand was Ma's tolerance of the situation. More than tolerance—she seemed to be encouraging Joanna instead of putting a stop to the entire messy business.

"Hannah!"

"Yes, Ma?"

"Hannah, you have been staring out the window for an age now. Are we to get no help from you at all?"

"I'm sorry, Ma," I answered. "I'm worried over Joanna."

"Of course you are, dear," Ma sympathized. "But Joanna knows her heart. And I trust her. She has always had good judgment and I do not believe she has lost it now." She paused. "I admit I would rather see her with a boy from here. But love does not always work out so neat and tidy. Not much in life does," she sighed. "Now please, go help Mrs. Phillips put her order together. She needs sugar, flour, and she wants a couple pickles from the barrel."

I nodded, and determined to put thoughts of Joanna aside. She would either see sense or she would not, and there was probably little I could do about it, especially with Ma being so unreasonable to boot.

I moved to assist Mrs. Phillips. The pickles in the barrel were a particular favorite of all our customers, as were Ma's other specialties from the old country—sauerkraut, pickled tomatoes, and pickled beets. In the winter it felt good to eat anything like that. I was scooping the pickles out of the barrel, trying to make sure I didn't drip on myself, when the postmaster came into the store, a smile on his old, creased face.

"Mrs. Green," he announced, "look what I have here for you. A letter from Mr. Green!"

Everyone in the shop stopped for a moment to greet this news with delight. Pa was a favorite in town, and everyone knew how important a job he had been given in the Confederacy—commissary for the entire region.

Ma's whole face lit up like a clear night with a full moon and a mess of stars. With trembling hands she opened the letter. Everyone waited, hoping she would share the news. She read for a moment, and then I could see the disappointment on her face as plain as when a moment before I had noted such delight.

"He writes that he is worried that he has had no word from us, although he fears it is because he is so on the move that our letters cannot reach him," Ma said. "So he knows nothing of what has happened here and has received none of my recent letters."

She sighed. We had all been hoping Pa would have received her letters and might even now be on his way home. I was terribly disappointed. He didn't know about Leon or our house or anything.

Ma read a portion of the letter aloud: "'You know, dear ones, that I often am a witness to the fighting. On one hot day in October I watched our boys fight the Federals in Corinth. And I have come to one conclusion.

"'Our hope that this war might end soon, dear family, I fear is a misplaced hope at best. To see those soldiers fight is to see men that will never surrender—on either side. No, this war will go on until one side is completely victorious over the other. And a complete victory can mean only one thing—the utter defeat and ruin of the other.

"'I am sorry if I do not write with my usual hope and good cheer, but I fear we must be prepared for even harder times ahead.'"

Ma looked up. "Then he writes of some personal matters," she explained.

Those in the store were grateful she had shared part of the letter with them, and told her as much. But the sense of unease I had felt as the day began was only increased by the tone of Pa's letter. Just as I was thinking that, the door flew open and two Federals roughly pushed their way past the customers.

"We are looking for the owner of this store," one said.

He was a short man with a bald head and small, beady eyes. His companion was far more pleasant in appearance, a tall young man with sandy hair and a hangdog kind of look.

My heart began to pound. Now what?

"I am the wife of the owner," Ma said, still clutching Pa's letter in her hand.

"And your husband," the little man said, his voice having an unpleasant nasal quality, "where is he?"

"Why, he is with the army."

"The Rebs?"

Ma drew herself up. "No, sir, the Confederate army."

"And his position?"

I was becoming nervous. Why all the questions? And why was Ma answering them? Wouldn't it be best to be quiet? But all the neighbors were around her and she could never stop herself boasting about Pa and his high position.

"He is a commissary," she said proudly.

"Then he is in defiance of the laws of the land. He has accepted a post in the rebel army, and under the law we may confiscate all of his goods."

Ma paled. Some of the customers in the store began to protest.

Miss Phillips said, "But you cannot. This is the shop closest to my home."

Only worried about herself, I thought.

Mr. Crane spoke up. "These folks, they've worked hard. They's law-abiding. You cain't just rob them like that."

The Yanks ignored them both. "As well, we are told that you are Jews," the small man stated.

"That is true," Ma said, her voice faint.

"General Grant issued Order Number Eleven some days ago. You shouldn't even be here. All Jews are ordered out of this area. You have until tomorrow at daybreak to prepare. Then you will leave this town escorted by troops moving to Memphis. From there you will be transported to Cairo, Illinois. The train tracks have been destroyed all around here, so if you possess a buggy of some sort, you may travel in that."

Henry walked up to them. "We will not go!" he declared. "This is our town. This is our store."

The little man, not much taller than him, stared at him and sneered. "You *will* go, young sir, or you and your entire family will be arrested. Which would you prefer?"

"You, sir," Henry declared, "are no better than scum on a pond."

He laughed. It was a nasty laugh. "And you," he said, "are nothing but a Jew." He motioned to the other soldier and they turned to leave. "We will be back within the hour for your goods," he said. And they were gone.

Everyone in the store stood silent. I was glad David had not been there to hear such things. And yet, I could not accept that I had heard those words spoken. I felt humiliated. I could not bear to look at anyone in the store. Would their eyes be full of pity? Or worse, would they begin to see me and my family as nothing but Jews? I stared at my shoes, afraid to glance up.

"Henry," Ma said, "go get Moses. Tell him what has happened. Tell him to bring the carriage; we must go back to the Hunters' house to pack." She seemed unsteady on her feet and suddenly sat down heavily. I ran over to her and took her hand. Slowly those in the store crept away as if embarrassed to face us.

"Don't worry, Ma," I said. "Don't worry."

I don't know why I kept saying that, except I didn't know what else to say. The dream, or rather nightmare, that had started two days earlier seemed to be going on and on, and there appeared to be no hope of waking from it. This could not be happening. Could it? Could it?

'　'　'

It didn't take long for Jule and Emily to pack all our belongings. Joanna had sent a note informing us that she was going along with Captain Mazer and the troops tomorrow. I had laughed when I read the note although there was nothing humorous in it. Wouldn't Joanna be surprised to discover that we were all going? How would she like her precious Union army then?

I sat with Eugenia and Mary in Eugenia's bedroom.

"They are barbarians!" Mary exclaimed. Mary was dressed all in black, in mourning for her brother George. "And what if Leon should be sent home?" she added. "The house destroyed. The store taken."

"You will take care of him, won't you, Mary?" I asked, forgetting to keep her secret. But she was so overwrought that she did not blink at my faux pas. And Eugenia did not seem to notice.

"Need you ask? Of course we will! But the Union soldiers are already at our plantation, taking what they want. We are to be treated little better than you."

I could not restrain myself. "That is not so. At least you are not being sent away because of your religion. Ma and Pa used to tell stories of how Jews were treated in Germany. Only the eldest sons were allowed to own property or even to marry! Jews were treated like a lower type of human. So Ma and Pa came to America, where everyone is treated equally. And we have been. Why, never, not until that Federal said it today, has anyone ever call me a Jew like that, as if it were an insult." I paused. "I was mortified." And even as I spoke those words I worried about whether my friends, despite their best intentions, might not slip into such a way of seeing.

I need not have worried.

Eugenia got that stern schoolmarm look on her face and said, "Hannah, I do not want to see your spirits taking such a beating from their evil talk. They can call you anything, but you needn't listen. Because remember who they are. And you just remember that you are a Southern lady, and they can call you what they wish, but you will always be a lady and they will always be the no-accounts that they are! Will you resolve to be strong?"

"I will," I answered, my heart full of gratitude for her steadfastness.

"You must swear," Eugenia demanded. She put her hand out and laid it on top of mine. Mary put hers on top of Eugenia's.

"We will all swear," Mary declared. "We will be brave and resolute."

"I swear," I said.

"I swear," Eugenia said.

"I swear," Mary said.

We hugged one another. "I could not possibly have better friends than the two of you," I whispered fervently.

"You'll be home, I mean, back here in no time," Eugenia predicted. "This order of General Grant's will never hold—that's what Pa says, and he knows everything."

"Did he say that?" I asked hopefully.

"He did. And he is never wrong."

I tried to take comfort in that. After all, there was little other comfort to be had.

Eugenia went over to her desk and returned with a book clutched in her hand. "I have just finished reading this," she said to me, "and now you must have it."

I took it from her. It was *The Woman in White*, by Wilkie Collins.

"Our heroine," Eugenia said, "has the most terrible tests and trials to her very sanity. I will not give away the end," she assured me (a practice we both abhorred), "but I will tell you that you will find it inspiring as well as suspenseful."

"Thank you, Eugenia," I said, and was afraid to speak further for fear of breaking down. I hoped I would have the strength I had pledged only moments earlier. I would have to be courageous. Why, then, did I feel instead like a small, scared child?

I looked back at Holly Springs and wondered if I would ever see it again. My family and I were crammed into the landau, bags and luggage all around us as well as on top. Joanna rode in a wagon up ahead, tending to Captain Mazer. We were near the end of a long line of Union soldiers who were moving toward Memphis, most on foot. They walked behind wagons filled with supplies, many of them, I thought bitterly, taken from my family's store. Moses drove the carriage, while Emily and Jule walked behind it, carrying their few possessions in packs on their backs.

"When Pa comes home, he's gonna worry something terrible 'bout us," David said. "He's gonna wonder where our house is. He's gonna wonder where his children is!"

"Are," I corrected him automatically. "Where his children *are*." I gave David a hug. "The Hunters have promised to have Pa live there, David. And they'll tell him where we are. And he'll come and bring us home, won't he, Ma?"

"Yes, dear," Ma said softly. "I believe he will. I worry, though, that he'll be very anxious for us. We must all stay strong, for his sake. Then when he finds us a great weight will be taken off his mind. He'll see we haven't suffered."

"Ma," Henry said, "I've been thinking that since you don't need me to help run the store anymore, I'd be of more use if I was in the army."

"No!"

"No!" I echoed.

"But, Ma, they need help. They ain't doing so well. And," he added, "it made me mad what the Yanks did to us! Real mad!"

"I'm angry too, Henry," Ma said. "But you are the only man we have with us now. Would you leave us women all alone?"

"What about me?" David demanded.

"You are a young man," Ma reassured him. "But we need your older brother, still."

Henry sighed, and nodded reluctantly. "As soon as we get back to Holly Springs then, Ma, all right?"

"We'll see, Henry."

I knew that Ma wanted to keep Henry at home until the war was over. He was only fourteen and far too young for such hard trials. Why, Eugenia had told me that her cousin from Oxford had bought his way out of the war, he had found it so brutish. And I knew Mary's brother George had been due to come home in just a few more weeks—his pa had found him a replacement, which you could do if you owned twenty or more slaves. People were starting to call it a poor man's war, but Henry saw none of that. He hated being home with the women. He couldn't be forcibly conscripted until age eighteen, but if he took it into his head to run off, as so many boys had done, there would be no way for Ma to stop him.

"Whoa there." Moses pulled the horse up short as we jolted to a sudden halt.

A Union soldier opened the carriage door.

"Please step out," he said.

"What is the meaning of this, sir?" Ma demanded.

"Please step out of the carriage," he repeated. He was a big man with a full black beard, and I didn't like the look of him at all.

"I would ask you to explain yourself," Ma said stubbornly. "My children are tired, as am I. Why do you want us out of the carriage?"

"You're the Jews," he said.

"We are Israelites," Ma agreed.

"We need this carriage. We have wounded who are walking. We'll put them in here."

"You are temporarily borrowing our carriage, for the wounded?" she asked, endeavoring to remain calm and polite.

"No," he said, "I am *taking* this carriage. You can walk. Get out. Or would you like my soldiers to pull you out?"

"Will you give us a receipt for the carriage?" Ma asked.

I don't know where Ma found the courage to talk to him that way, but she no longer seemed afraid. She didn't look weak or faint—she simply seemed enraged.

"I will see you dead first," the soldier shouted. "Out of the carriage, woman, you try my patience!"

I gasped, feeling as though he had sent a dagger through my heart, speaking to Ma so.

"Children," Ma said, "we will walk."

We got out of the carriage, and Moses began to pull

our trunks from the back and the top and to empty the insides, too.

Ma drew herself up. "And how will we carry our trunks?" she asked.

The soldier looked at her for a moment. Then he called a couple other soldiers over.

"Burn these," he ordered. He turned back to Ma. "You won't have to worry about carrying them."

"You *cannot*!" I exclaimed. "My books are in there. My studies! My clothes! My dolls!"

"Sergeant," said one of the soldiers, "allow the children to take a few things."

"Take what you can carry," the sergeant agreed. "Burn the rest," he ordered his men, and he got on his horse and rode off.

Ma sagged against the carriage once the horrible man was gone.

"Ma," I said, putting my arm around her waist, "are you all right?"

"I think so, dear," she replied.

"You showed grit, Ma," Henry said, his voice full of admiration.

"You were wonderful!" David said with a grin.

"Not so wonderful," she said, straightening herself up. "They are to take everything! Quickly, Moses, open the trunks. Children, make bundles out of the linen in my trunk and put what you can carry in the bundles. Moses and Emily and Jule will carry some as well."

Just when I thought nothing could get worse, it seemed we were to be stripped of everything. I was proud, though, of the way Ma had talked to that lout, and I resolved to try and stay strong, just as I had promised my friends. Still, tears burned behind my eyes as I surveyed my trunk—all I had left in the world.

What should I choose? I put my jewelry in my beaded purse and placed that first on the ground onto the piece of cloth I would later tie into a bundle. I chose the book *The Woman in White*, naturally, as it was a treasured gift from Eugenia; my books of poetry; my Austen. I simply couldn't carry even those few; they would be too heavy. So I put them in a second bundle for Jule to carry. I included my three small dolls and my three statuettes. I chose two pairs of stockings, two pairs of underclothes, a skirt, a blouse, and a nightdress. My extra crinoline was too large for the bundle, so I would have to make do with the one I had on.

I looked through my trunk one last time. The catechism. I wasn't sure why at the time, but I decided to take that as well. Somehow I suppose I saw it as part of my pa. I included a pair of warm gloves and an extrawarm scarf. I was wearing my coat and had a muff and toque on. I put the muff away. It would be of no use as we walked. I stared at my music box, my brushes, my jewelry box—I would have to watch as they went up in flames.

I didn't know I was weeping until I tasted the tears that were coursing down my cheeks. My breath came in short puffs, and I could see it in the cold morning air. Why did that soldier hate my family? I couldn't understand it. What was *wrong* with being an Israelite? Surely we were the same as everyone else. We even looked the same. If someone hadn't betrayed us, no one would have known that we were Jews. So why hate us?

I stopped for a moment to think. Who *did* inform on us? How *did* those soldiers know we were Israelites? Could Captain Mazer have given us away? I doubted it. He said he would protect us. And he did seem fond of Joanna.

Private Katz? I doubted that, too. But perhaps one of *their* friends who knew he was wooing a Southern girl. My breath caught in my throat. Why, Captain Mazer's friends would be as against the match as I was. But how *dare* they? Joanna was perfect. Any man would be lucky to have her. Had it been a misguided attempt to separate them by someone who saw all Southerners as bad? *No different,* I thought, *than the way I see all Northerners.* I suddenly felt my head begin to spin. But they *were* all bad. . . . Yet, could a people as a group *be* all bad?

"Hannah," Ma asked, "are you ill?"

"No, Ma," I replied as I tried to shake off my thoughts. "My mind was wandering."

"Well, bring it back," Ma said. "Henry probably needs your help. You know how boys are."

I went over to Henry. "Can I help you?"

"If I had a rifle," Henry hissed, "I would've shot him cold dead. Instead we have to be humiliated like that! I wanted to say something, but Ma was pinching me the whole time!"

"Was she?" I couldn't help a small smile. "That explains why you were so quiet."

"I'm gonna run away, Hannah. And then I'm gonna come back and shoot that soldier!"

"Henry," I said (although I wished he *could* shoot him dead right then and there), "you are needed here. You may not have said anything, but just having a man with us is a protection. Would you want us walking now without you to protect us?"

"No," Henry admitted. "I wouldn't."

The troops had continued to pass us by on the road as all this happened. The soldiers overseeing us motioned for us to fall in behind them when our bundles were tied and ready. We did so. I was just as glad to be forced to move, as I couldn't bear to see my belongings disappearing into the flames. Our servants took the heavy bundles, hunching under their weight as they walked.

We were on Pigeon Roost Road, and I could see that soon we'd be in the town of Red Banks. I wondered where would we sleep. We wouldn't reach Memphis until late the next day, if we were lucky. I walked beside Henry and asked him the question that was still burning for an answer.

"Why do they hate us?" I said, forcing myself not to look back, not to see the fire.

Ma overheard. "Hannah, think of the history your pa has taught you. People have hated Israelites for thousands of years. Pharaoh kept us in bondage for hundreds of years before Moses took us to freedom. In Spain we were thrown out of the country or made to convert. In Germany they passed laws against us. When anything goes wrong, people look for someone to blame. Someone different. They see us. And they blame us. Calling us profiteers. We know it isn't true. But they have to blame someone."

"But that's what I don't understand," I said. "We aren't different. I am *just* the same as my friends."

"Well, dear," Ma answered, "there is no logic to this kind of thinking. It will never make any sense no matter how hard you try to understand it."

"Ma, Ma!" It was Joanna. She was running toward us. "Ma," she said, panting slightly from running so hard, "I heard them talking, laughing, up there about what they did. Are you all right?"

"I cannot say we are all right," Ma answered. "We are not physically injured yet, although I am concerned about this long walk. But for the children to have to hear such things . . . no, we are *not* all right."

Joanna hugged each of us, even me. In that moment she seemed to have forgotten that we had ever quarreled.

"Jonathan is so distressed. He says he will resign his commission if the order is not revoked."

"How is he?" Ma asked.

I wondered at her being able to concern herself with a Yank after what we had just experienced.

"A little feverish," she answered as she took up the pace beside me and took my hand. "Jonathan is distressed that you and I have quarreled over him. He has asked me to make up with you. I am willing if you are."

I was far too angry even to consider such a thing. "I cannot make it up with you, Joanna, because *he* wishes us to. *He* is one of *them*. And look what they have reduced us to. Look!"

Joanna dropped my hand. "I told him you would never change your way of seeing. You are fixed in it and determined. Your view of the world must seem as a safe haven to you." Joanna paused and then said, "It is *not* a safe haven, Hannah, only an illusion you trick yourself with."

"Stop lecturing me!" I exclaimed. I could stand being near her no longer. I walked over to Henry and fell in beside him.

"Henry," I said, "tell me what you will do when you are a soldier."

. . .

We were allowed to stop briefly for dinner. The Hunters had packed a dinner basket, which Emily had saved from the fire. It was a sumptuous feast of cold meats, sweet-potato pie, fresh corn bread, and peppermint sticks and homemade candies. A flask of tea washed it all down. I found that I was famished after the long walk, and I gratefully gobbled down every bit of food Emily put in front of me.

The lull was brief, though, and soon we were walking again. David could simply not keep up, so Joanna asked Captain Mazer to intervene. He arranged for both David and Ma to ride in the covered wagon with him, while Joanna walked farther back with Henry, the servants, and me.

We began passing a series of farmhouses that were close to the road. At each house the Yanks sent in small raiding parties of about twenty men, along with a horse and wagon. They'd enter a house and within minutes come out laden with goods. *No doubt,* I thought, *General Grant will make all the neighbors around pay for those destroyed supplies.* I recognized some of the homes as belonging to families we knew.

"They're going to the Johnson farm," Henry exclaimed. "They better watch—"

A hail of balls whizzed all around us cutting off Henry's words. A soldier just in front of us took a hit in the arm, and blood spattered all over my dress. As I looked down at the grisly mess I felt myself being pulled to the ground. I turned my head to see it was Moses who had pulled me down. He had grabbed Joanna at the same time.

"Get down, Henry!" he shouted.

Henry threw himself down. "That's my friend Billy, I bet," Henry yelled. "He won't let those Yanks steal from him! And Ike, too, I'll wager!"

"Young'uns, this way!" Moses shouted over the screams of the soldiers and the agonizing shrieks of the wounded. He dropped down on his belly, pushing us ahead of him. We ended up in a shallow gully on the far side of the road from the farmhouses, but so did many of the troops as they took up positions to return fire. Someone yelled an order and all around us the soldiers let loose a fearsome barrage on the Johnson farm just opposite, not more than a few hundred yards away. The sound was almost deafening. I couldn't think at all what to do, so I put my hands over my ears and tried to make myself as small as possible by curling into a ball.

"Hannah," Joanna shouted above the din, "come here! This man needs help."

I looked up. I could see that the injured soldier had been dragged down into the gully. No one was ministering to him, so Joanna had obviously crawled over to see what she could do.

I had no intention of helping any injured Yank. I began to crawl away, reasoning that the farther I was from the fighting, the better off I would be.

"Just where in the dickens do you think you're going?" a Federal screamed at me.

"Somewhere safe!" I screamed.

"You go help with the wounded like you was just asked or nowhere'll be safe for you!"

How *dare* he? Who did he think he was, ordering me about! I continued to crawl away, when suddenly I felt something in my back. It was the barrel of a rifle. "I mean it," he growled.

Even Yanks don't shoot women, I thought. But the feel of the muzzle on my back was a nasty shock. I decided not to test his resolve. Reluctantly I crawled over to Joanna.

There was gunfire all around us, men screaming orders, and Joanna was behaving as if we were in no danger.

"Rip some of your petticoat," she said briskly, "so I can wrap his arm." She had already ripped hers and had used it to wrap his hand.

I was about to object, but at that moment the wounded man turned toward me. Why, he looked no older than Leon, with huge blue eyes wide open in pain and shock. His arm had been ripped by the ball, which had taken off a big chunk of flesh. I pulled up my skirt and tore my petticoat, handing it to Joanna without a word of protest. Joanna wound it around the boy's arm, then tried to comfort him.

I turned to see Moses hanging on to Henry, who was trying to get away.

"Let me go!" Henry shouted.

"No, young master, you'll stay right here, you will. This be a fight you can't win!"

I scrambled over to them.

"That is plain foolish, Henry," I scolded him. "There must be a thousand men here. Your friends are committing an act of pure folly. They will get themselves killed or taken prisoner, and then when they are old enough to enlist, they will not be able to. Is that helping your country?"

"I can't worry about my country," Henry exclaimed. "They are my friends and they need help."

"Does it help a friend to get yourself killed? Will you leave them with that burden—that they were the cause of your death? Because death or capture, Henry, it will be. Look around!"

I held my breath. Had I convinced him?

Henry stopped struggling with Moses. "You are right, Sister," he sighed.

"Hannah, I need your help!" It was Joanna again. I turned and crawled back to her. The gunfire was lessening now, and the order was given for some of the men to take the farm. Another volley was let loose by the Federals to cover their troops. I thought I might go deaf.

"Hannah, he needs something for the pain," Joanna said. "You must find one of the surgeons up ahead."

"Why me?" I protested. "Let one of these men go!"

The same soldier was suddenly there again. Didn't he have some fighting to do?

He answered my unasked question. "I got my eye on you," he said. "Trying to run like that—the sergeant told me to watch you all. Said you couldn't be trusted because you're Jews. I never met a Jew, so I didn't know if he was right, but I guess he was. Your sister, she's acting just fine like though, so you listen to her. The boy needs a doc, and we're a little busy here with other concerns."

I stared at the soldier, so stunned that for a moment I *couldn't* move. He mistrusted me because I was a Jew.

"Now," he bellowed. "Not tomorrow!"

I scrambled away, moving along the gully. I had to pass Moses on the way. When I told him what I'd been ordered to do, he said, "That's more of a job for a man, ain't it, Miss Hannah? You go help your sister with the nursing, and Master Henry and myself will find a doctor. Anyways, in all the confusion I don't know what's happened to Emily and Jule and your ma and Master David, so we'll go see."

Henry seemed keen on such an expedition and willingly went with Moses. I crawled back to Joanna and the repugnant Federal. Before he could holler at me again, I explained that my servant had gone to fetch a doctor.

"Your *slave*, you mean," he sneered.

"It was *his* idea, not mine," I objected.

"Then make yourself useful here," he snapped. "I'm goin' after my unit—we got some cleanin' up to do."

Indeed, the firing had lessened and the gully was quickly emptying of men. Soon only the wounded boy and we two girls were left.

"What is your name?" Joanna asked.

"William," he replied.

"Tell me about your family, William," she said.

"My pa died at Bull Run," he said. "All the rest at home are sisters, three of them."

"So there'll be lots of fussing over you when you get back home, won't there?" Joanna smiled.

"They like to spoil me a touch," he admitted. He grimaced suddenly, wracked with pain.

"Well, now, soldier, I'm a sister too," Joanna said, "and I can tell you that they'll be peeved with you if you don't get better. So you fight hard, you hear?"

He nodded. "Can you recite to me from the Good Book?" the boy whispered.

"Of course," Joanna agreed. "I will recite a psalm."

"I'd be mighty grateful," the boy sighed. "In case I'm with the good Lord soon."

"William," Joanna said. "You think of your dear sisters and how they'll be pining for you. The good Lord will wait awhile longer."

She began to recite to the boy. We'd memorized many psalms in our studies with Pa. The one she recited was one of my favorites.

"God is my shepherd. I shall need nothing. He always

will cause me to recline in a habitation of tender verdure, and gently bend my steps beside soft rivulets. He will re-create my soul, and for His name's sake, He will have me led in the paths of rectitude. Should I ever walk in the valley of deadly shade, I would fear no evil; for Thou art with me, Thy staff and Thy support are my comfort. Thou preparest a table for me, also in the presence of my adversaries. Thou gracest my head with abundant oil. My cup overfloweth. Only goodness and grace will follow me all the days of my life, and I shall sit many days in the house of God."

"C'mon, boys, here he is. Lift him out of here onto the wagon."

I jumped. I had been listening so closely that I hadn't heard the soldiers as they came up behind us. I turned to see an older man followed by two Federals.

William spoke to Joanna. "Thank you, ma'am," he said. "You've been an angel of mercy. I'll remember you in my prayers as long as the good Lord lets me stay here."

"And I will pray for you," Joanna promised. "God keep you, William," she called as they carried him off.

I couldn't help but feel sorry for the poor boy, even though he was a Yankee. He seemed so sweet. I regretted that I had not wanted to help him. Being a Southern lady surely meant taking care of those less fortunate, whoever they happened to be. I turned to Joanna to say as much, when I noticed that she and I were completely alone in the gully. Joanna took my hand and drew me forward onto the road, where we saw a large group of Federals across from us, wagons full of goods, taking away prisoners. Behind them a small group on horseback came galloping up, as if to catch up to the main unit, which was far ahead, almost out of sight.

We moved over to the side of the road to let them pass, when one of the men pulled up his horse and raised his hand for the others to stop. He leaped off his mount and said, "Well, well, what have we here? Reb spies? Why would you two ladies be walking along this road all alone?"

"Sir," Joanna said, "we are traveling with the column up ahead, toward Memphis."

"Now, why would that be?"

He was an older man with a gray beard and a stern, suspicious expression. I did not at all like being called a spy. It made me nervous, as did being all alone with those soldiers.

"We have been ordered to leave our home in Holly Springs because we are Israelites," Joanna replied.

The man looked us over. "Well, that is your story. But it seems to me more likely that you are spies! Look at the state of you—looks to me like you've been in a fight. Very suspicious. We have a good jail in Memphis for spies!"

"Sir, I beg you," Joanna exclaimed, "send one of your men ahead to the soldiers. They will vouch for us. The blood is from the skirmish that just happened."

"My sister nursed one of your men," I exclaimed indignantly. "That is how she became bloody!"

He gazed at us for a moment. "Have you pledged your allegiance to the Union?" the soldier demanded.

"Why no, sir," Joanna said.

"Certainly not!" I declared.

"Well, then, perhaps you would like to do so?"

"Never!" I exclaimed before Joanna could speak. Joanna threw me a fierce look but I didn't care. Pledge allegiance? Why, I'd prefer roasting over hot coals.

"You will accompany us to Memphis, then," the soldier stated.

"But, sir, we will run into the group ahead at Red Banks or Byhalia and then we can sort this out!" Joanna protested.

"No, miss, we are not going that way."

"What do you mean?"

"We are cutting down a small side road up ahead, which will take us more directly to Memphis."

That sent a wave of panic right through me. We were to travel with no protection—suddenly Captain Mazer and Private Katz seemed like guardian angels. And we were to be taken to jail. Jail! My heart began to pound in terror. I slipped my hand into Joanna's. Her hand squeezed mine reassuringly. How glad I was at that moment to be with my older sister.

"Sir," Joanna said, "you have upset both me and my sister. In fact . . . in fact, I feel quite faint. . . ." She squeezed my hand again. Suddenly I understood. Without wasting a moment, I swooned, then fell to the ground.

Quickly Joanna bent over me. "Henry is about to come looking for us," she whispered. "We *must* stay on this road."

I kept my eyes closed and made no movement. I was

impressed with Joanna and her quick thinking. It made me feel a little less afraid, because we were at least *doing* something.

Joanna then slumped to the ground herself, saying, "Sir, I am afraid you have made us both quite ill."

"Luckily I have a surgeon with us," he replied. "Major, we have two ladies who seem to be indisposed."

I heard movement and began getting nervous again. Of all the bad luck—a doctor would quickly discover our deception.

No sooner had I thought that than the pungent whiff of smelling salts made me bolt upright. It was quite impossible to pretend they were not under your nose.

"There," said an older man, who looked at me kindly. "Better?"

I nodded. And then I heard a sound that was pure music to my ears.

"Hannah! Joanna!"

We turned to see Henry running down the road, Moses right beside him.

"Henry!" Joanna and I struggled to our feet.

"And who are you?" the soldier said, as Henry approached us.

"Henry Green, sir," Henry replied. "These are my sisters."

"And are you a spy too?" the soldier asked.

"I hope you are not accusing my sisters of such a thing. They are quite innocent!"

"So *you* say," the soldier replied. "But I think you will *all* come with us to Memphis, and to jail."

Henry looked like he was about to attack the soldier with his bare hands. Moses stepped in front of him.

"Sir," he said, "they are telling you the truth."

"And who are you?"

"Moses," he answered.

"He's our slave!" Henry exclaimed, pushing him aside. "I'm the man here. You may talk to *me*."

The soldier ignored Henry. "Moses, how do these people treat you?"

Moses looked surprised. "They treat me well," he replied.

"But do they treat you so well that you choose to stay with them rather than choosing to be free?"

Moses looked sharply at him. "What do you mean?"

"I mean you could join the contraband camp at Grand Junction or Corinth. You could be free. You could simply walk away, right now."

Moses would never *do that*, I thought, full of contempt for such an outlandish idea. I waited for him to disabuse the lout. Instead Moses said, "Would I be protected?"

"If you choose to leave, one of the men will put you with troops going there. Naturally it would not be safe for you to go on your own."

"No, sir, it sure wouldn't," Moses answered. "Why, over on the Clark plantation a friend of mine died from the lash when they caught him trying to get to the contraband camp."

No doubt that was the lashing I had witnessed. And I had likened it to a spanking. Now I really *did* feel dizzy. I hadn't given that poor soul a second thought, had I?

"His name was Thom," Moses continued. "Been a foot-man in their service for twenty-some years. Had three children that lived, was a gentle soul. They was fond of him—but they killed him easy as killing a dog that's got the sickness, and maybe he was a good dog, but now he has to be killed."

"We must be going," the soldier said. "What's your decision, then?"

"I'll be staying with 'em for now," Moses answered.

For now? Surely he couldn't be considering leaving, I thought.

"If you vouch for these Rebs, then I'll let them go," the soldier said.

"I vouch for 'em." Moses nodded. "They ain't no spies."

The soldier looked at us. "The only reason I'm letting you go," he said, "is because your *slave* has said you've treated him well. I warn you though: If he tries to leave, don't stand in his way."

I felt relief wash all over me. We would not have to go to jail. And that Yank had no idea who he was dealing with. Moses would never leave us. He had no doubt answered the Yank that way because he felt that's what the Yank wanted to hear.

"Skedaddle, then," the soldier ordered. "Best get caught up with the troops up ahead."

I turned to Henry. "Is Ma all right? And David?"

"They are fine, just worried over you both," Henry answered. He gave the soldier a worried look and said, "I suggest we do skedaddle before someone changes his mind."

We hurried down the road to catch up with the others.

I woke up suddenly with a cramp in my calf that was so excruciating I cried aloud, waking everyone in the room.

Ma, Joanna, and I were sharing a bed in a small hotel room in the town of Byhalia. Ma massaged the leg once I had pointed to where the cramp was, and slowly the pain diminished. Henry and David had been asleep on the carpet on the floor, but they woke up grumbling when I made such a racket.

I had been so exhausted the night before that I had fallen fast asleep as soon as I lay down. The Union troops, anxious to reach Memphis by Christmas Eve, had marched at quick pace for eight hours, with us desperately trying to keep up.

The room was becoming light, and I knew that we would soon be on the road again. Just then there was a soft knock at the door. Henry scrambled over and opened it. Moses stood there. He had the bundles he had carried the day before, along with those Emily had carried.

"Missus, may I speak with you?"

"Of course, Moses, come in," Ma said.

He stood awkwardly by the door and paused for a moment. He put down the bundles. "Missus," he said, "I ain't going with you no farther."

Ma looked puzzled. "I don't understand." She paused. "Is it that blackguard Union soldier? Is he taking you to work for him?"

"Not exactly, missus. I been thinking on this since the soldier we ran into yesterday talked to me about being free. So I went and talked to the sergeant. He was real nice to me. He told me that I could go to the contraband camp in Grand Junction under the protection of some troops he be sending there. Emily can go too, as a cook."

Again Ma looked confused. "But you cannot simply go, Moses. You belong to Mr. Green. He has not freed you, not the last I know."

"He ain't, that's true. But the army has."

"How could you leave us, Moses?" I burst out. "Who will take care of us?" I couldn't believe he was saying this.

Moses gave me a sympathetic look. "Why, Miss Hannah, you will have to take care of yourself," he replied. "I'm sorry, missus," he said, turning back to Ma. "You never treated me bad. Only good. But it ain't the same as being free. I gotta go now." And before Ma could say anything more he had turned and was walking away.

"I forbid you to go!" Henry called after him.

But Moses did not even slow down in response to Henry's order.

"Stop him," Ma exclaimed.

But how? We couldn't stop him physically. Moses was a big, strong man.

"I will," I said. "I will try to persuade him." I hurried from the room. Moses had just reached the landing at the bottom of the stairs when I caught up with him. He turned and patiently waited for me to speak.

"I thought you cared for us, Moses. We care for you."

"Miss Hannah," Moses said, "how much could you care for a slave? How much could you care for something you *own*?"

"But you aren't a thing," I protested. "You've always helped Pa and he trusts you. How will he feel when he hears you've left us here all alone?"

Moses looked me in the eye then. I was taken aback. He'd never done that before. His eyes were black as coal and deeply intense.

"Can you imagine what it is like, Miss Hannah, not to be treated as a equal human being?"

I thought for a moment. "Yes, I can! Because that's the way the Union has treated us the last few days. But that's different. We *are* equal. We *are* the same. I'm sorry, Moses, but the Negro race is not the same as the white race."

"And how you know that, Miss Hannah?"

"Why, everyone knows that."

"If everyone knows that, why do so many in the North believe we *is* equal? Why do they believe slavery is bad?"

"They are misinformed," I replied.

"Are they? Or are *you*?"

I was so surprised by the audacity of his remark that for a moment I couldn't respond.

"You must admit, Miss Hannah, it ain't accepted by everyone in the world. So one side must be wrong." He paused. "The sergeant, it's funny, ain't it, that he hates Jews but he likes Negroes. You think you could convince him you are the same as he is? You are *his* equal? No, you couldn't, 'cause he has it in his head you's bad. All of you's bad. And, Miss Hannah, you have it in your head all of *us* is inferior. If I'm so inferior, how is it I can run your pa's store when he ain't there? How is it I can read and write so good? And, Miss Hannah, I'll tell you somethin' else"—his voice grew fierce—"I loved a girl once. I loved her and we wanted to marry and have a family. But slaves ain't allowed to do that! Well, I'll tell you, I'd make a good daddy and a good husband. To you I may look old, but I'm just reaching my thirty-fifth year. And one day I'll get married and I'll have a family. Because as of today I am free.

"You just imagine, Miss Hannah—what if they hated you as Jews and decided you should be no better than slaves? What if they made *you* all into slaves? Wouldn't you still be *you*? With all your feeling and with all your brains, too? But they wouldn't see you like that, would they?"

"It's not the same," I said, but Ma's words to me about Pharaoh and how we Israelites *were* slaves in Egypt for four hundred years came back to me. "It's not the same," I repeated, almost to myself. "The soldiers who hate Jews are ignorant. They are stupid."

"And you hate Negroes because . . . ?"

"But I don't hate you!"

"No, you love me so much you think I need to be bought and sold like you would a horse. Miss Hannah, I got to go now. I'm gonna fight for the Union. I'm gonna be a soldier."

He was going to take up arms against his own family? Leon and Simon? Before I could think of what to say, he spoke again.

"I'm fond of you and your whole family, I truly am," he said. "I hope one day you'll understand what I just tried to tell you."

He turned to go.

I had to think. What would Eugenia do? She would

remind me that I am a lady and that if you *demand* respect you will get respect.

I drew myself up as tall as I could. "How dare you turn your back to me that way!" I declared. "I insist you remain with us."

"Good-bye, Miss Hannah," he answered over his shoulder. "Good luck to you."

He walked out of the front door of the small hotel without a backward glance. I ran to the door and opened it in time to see him walk away with Emily. Emily hadn't even bothered to say good-bye! Why, she'd cooked for us all those years; she'd let me help oftentimes if I begged her, and although she was short-tempered if I spilled a bit of flour or sugar, she'd always seemed . . . I stopped. Happy? I had never before thought about whether or not Emily or Moses was happy. They were slaves, after all. I leaned against the door and watched them walk off into the morning mist.

Was there a comparison between what was happening to me and my family and what Moses had experienced? Ordinarily I would have dismissed the thought out of hand. But nothing about that moment was ordinary. I was exhausted. My world had been shattered. Nothing made sense. Instead of ignoring his words as one part of me wanted to do, another part wondered if there was any truth to it.

Moses in love? I'd never thought of him that way. And he'd spoken so tenderly of being a husband and a father. If it were true, as I'd always believed, that Negroes were not the equals of whites, how *was* it that Moses had been clever enough to run Pa's business? And although he spoke in an uneducated way, he would have to be very smart, in fact, to teach himself reading and writing. Perhaps he'd even had to hide his abilities until Pa bought him, because some slave owners would kill a slave for learning to read and write. And they would suspect a slave that talked too fancy. Why had none of that ever occurred to me before?

Just then a soldier came walking toward the hotel through the mist Moses had disappeared into. Quickly he was at the door. "I'm looking for the Green family."

"I am Hannah Green."

"We leave shortly. Get your family ready and meet us on the road out of Byhalia."

I nodded my head. I was just about to turn around when, much to my own surprise, I said to the soldier, who couldn't have been more than a few years older than me, "Why are you fighting?"

His eyebrows rose up and he took a closer look at me. "Why do you ask?"

I shrugged, suddenly embarrassed. What kind of Southern lady struck up conversations with complete strangers? And yet I had never heard a Federal explain why the war had to happen. Naturally it was not discussed when Captain Mazer came to call. It seemed safer to ask a stranger.

"I'm fightin'," he answered, "because I love my country and I'm willin' to die to keep it together."

"You see Mississippi as part of your country?"

"I do. I see all the reb states as part of my country. And

if we let you go, why, soon some Northern state'll go because it don't like some law, and then another, and soon—well, we won't *be* a country no more."

"But we want to be our own country!" I objected. "Why can't you let us?"

"A country based on slaves," he snorted. "One out of four in bondage, I been told."

"But the war isn't *about* that," Hannah said. "We just don't want the North telling us our business!"

"You believe that if you want," the young fellow said, shaking his head. "I'm sure I won't be changing your mind and it's a waste of my breath to try. My pa always says that once people are set in their ways, well, usually they stay set. And I believe from what I've seen since I joined up he had the truth of that. Now, you go hurry up your family."

He wasn't even willing to argue with me, he thought so little of me. I began to object, when he waved at me as if I were a pesky fly or mosquito. "Get off with you," he said. "Quick like."

I turned and ran up the stairs.

"We must get ready to go," I said as I entered the room.

"Hannah," Ma said, "what did Moses say? Will he stay?"

I shook my head. "Both he and Emily are gone."

"After Pa has been so good to them." Ma shook her head. "What about Jule?"

"She didn't leave with them," I said.

"She has probably chosen to stay, then," Ma said. "I'm sure Moses would have asked her to go with them. Let us be thankful for small mercies." She gave me a sharp look. "What is it, dear? You really look unwell."

"I've been having some crazy thoughts, that's all, Ma. I'm going to try to put them all out of my head."

"You do that, dear," Ma said. "We have enough troubles. Let's get ourselves safely to Memphis, and perhaps Rabbi Tuska can help us."

"Yes, Ma."

And I did have more practical things to worry about—my feet, for instance, which hurt like the dickens. And the extra load of bundles that Moses and Emily had been carrying, which we now had to manage on our own. Jule came up to help us get ready and said not a word about Moses, carrying on as if everything were normal.

Even with Jule carrying as much as she could, though, it quickly became obvious that the bundles would be too heavy for us, and so Ma told us that we would have to leave almost everything behind. Joanna found Private Katz and asked him for help. She returned to us with a smile on her face.

"He has arranged to get all our bundles put on a wagon, so we don't have to carry anything," she said.

This, at least, was a huge relief, and we left the room looking forward to a far less arduous walk. And we didn't have the unthinkable task of having to part with the very last of our things. David had kept the menorah in his pack, for instance, and saw it as some kind of talisman that he must have at all costs. And I felt the same about everything I had with me.

When we got back on the road, I walked with Henry

and Joanna. Ma and David rode along with Captain Mazer. I didn't speak to Joanna, or Henry really. It's not that I was lost in thought—it was more that my mind was in a state of emptiness. I couldn't seem to hold a thought for more than a second or two.

The Federal troops, marching four astride ahead of us, were singing as loud as they could. I had never heard the song before, as it was a Yankee tune, and I couldn't help but listen now.

> "Yes, We'll rally round the flag,
> Boys, we'll rally once again,
> Shouting the battle-cry of Freedom,
> We will rally from the hillside, we'll gather from the plain,
> Shouting the battle-cry of Freedom.
> The Union forever,
> Hurray! boys, Hurrah!
> Down with the traitor, up with the star;
> While we rally round the flag, boys, rally once again,
> Shouting the battle-cry of Freedom.
> We are springing to the call of our brothers gone before,
> Shouting the battle-cry of Freedom;
> And we'll fill the vacant ranks with a million freemen more,
> Shouting the battle-cry of Freedom.
> We will welcome to our numbers the loyal, true and brave,
> Shouting the battle-cry of Freedom;
> And altho' they may be poor, not a man shall be a slave,
> Shouting the battle-cry of Freedom.
> So we're springing to the call from the East and the West,
> Shouting the battle-cry of Freedom;

> And we'll hurl the rebel crew from the land we love the best,
> Shouting the battle-cry of Freedom."

* * *

It made me shiver. And the way they sang about slaves—over and over I'd been told the war wasn't about that. Then why were they singing about it?

When we stopped to eat and Jule had put out all the food for us, I turned to her and asked, "Where are you from, Jule?"

"From, missy?"

"Yes, where were you before you came to us?"

"Before your pa bought me, you mean?"

"Yes."

"Why, I was over at the Middletons' plantation."

"Were you born there?"

"Yes, missy, I was born there."

"And are your parents still there?"

"My ma is. My pa got sold out Georgia way. Ma cries 'bout that every night."

"She misses him?"

"Well, what do you think?"

"I . . . I . . . I don't know. Why did they sell you?"

"I couldn't do no right there. They's so strict it made my nerves go all crazy like, and I'd just get near a teacup or some such and I'd break it. And I wasn't too good in the field, neither. They whupped me all the time, but it didn't help. Made my nerves worse. Your pa, he was over once, and he saw me get in trouble—next thing you know he bought me! The Master Middleton was sure happy."

I looked at Ma.

"You know what your pa is like," Ma said, shrugging her shoulders. "He knew she looked like a good girl, and they give such terrible beatings there. . . ."

"They did," Jule agreed. "So I would *never* leave you like Moses did! I'll stay with you, missus," she said to Ma. "Don't you worry. And those slaves who run off—why, they gonna starve to death, I bet!"

"Why, you have no choice, girl!" Henry exclaimed. "What's gotten into them? Hannah, you encourage her to be forward."

"Henry, she's simply talking to her," Joanna snapped.

"Let us all eat our lunch," Ma said. "We have a long walk ahead of us yet."

, , ,

It had started to rain, lightly at first, but it quickly turned into a downpour. I had fortunately kept my umbrella, and so had the others, but that didn't keep my boots from leaking and my crinoline from getting wet. My skirt felt like it weighed hundreds of pounds as I dragged it along. The road quickly became muddy, and my teeth began to chatter from the cold and damp. Ma was riding up ahead in the wagon with David and Captain Mazer. Henry took my arm, and Jule took hold of Joanna to help her walk. In this manner we trudged along, completely miserable, unable to talk or even to think.

We passed through Olive Branch, then Gum Grove, and finally Nonconnah Creek, but were not allowed even to stop for a rest. Night was coming on when the regiment finally pulled up just outside of Memphis.

The soldiers began their preparation for Christmas Eve celebrations. I saw tobacco being passed around and heard the men calling for the whiskey punch. Soon small groups began to form, and the men began to sing hymns, carols, and songs like "Home Sweet Home."

Ma rejoined us. "We must ask permission from the sergeant, who seems to be in charge of us, for Henry to leave," Ma said. "I'm sure that if Henry goes to Temple Children of Israel and finds Rabbi Tuska, he will locate somewhere for us to stay tonight."

"I don't see why we can't remain in Memphis," Henry said. "We are out of Grant's territory now. The army should let us stay here."

"I believe you are right," Ma agreed. "If the rabbi can find a place for us to stay, we are close to Holly Springs from here and could easily return if and when the order is rescinded. You must go and ask that wretched man for his permission."

Henry returned within minutes, the hated sergeant riding behind him on his horse.

"Madam," the sergeant said, "apparently you are under a mistaken impression."

"And what is that, sir?" Ma replied. "That you are a gentleman?"

The sergeant scowled, but did not respond to the insult. "General Grant's orders are clear. All Jews are being sent to Cairo, Illinois, to be processed. There you will receive the necessary papers to travel outside General Grant's jurisdiction. I suspect you will be sent wherever a transport is going at the time."

"But we are out of his district now, are we not?" Ma asked.

"I have orders to take you to Cairo and I will follow my orders," the sergeant snapped. "There is an end of it!"

"And for tonight? You can see my children are cold and wet. We must at least be allowed a good night's rest and a change into dry clothes," Ma demanded.

"I'm afraid I cannot allow that. Memphis is a large town where you could easily get lost and try to avoid me. You can spend the night here with my troops, or I can try to put you on a ship or train leaving for Cairo now."

"This is barbarous!" Ma objected.

"Sir," Joanna said, "I have been nursing Captain Mazer and some of the wounded. Where are they going?"

"They are to board a ship that will stop in Cairo, in Paducah, then on up the Ohio River."

"Will they stop in Cincinnati?" Joanna said.

"Yes."

"And that is out of General Grant's territories, is it not?"

"Yes."

"And would we be allowed to go there?"

"Yes, you would, *after* you have been processed in Cairo."

Joanna turned to Ma. "Ma, please, let us go with them. We can stay with Uncle Jacob there. Captain Mazer is reviving slowly and can offer us some support on this journey. I suggest, not only for my sake but for all of our sakes, that we travel together."

Ma considered for a moment, then nodded.

"Follow the captain's wagon, then," ordered the sergeant.

I was so disappointed that I was tempted to sink down into the ground and give up altogether. All that had kept me going over the last few hours was the thought of a warm, dry bed, a hot meal, and the good wishes and sympathy of Rabbi Tuska and others. Our family often traveled to Memphis for services, especially for the High Holidays and when the boys had been called to the Torah. I had been hoping for tender words and indignation over our plight. Now we were to be shipped off into the night.

What was the matter with me, I wondered, that I could even *question* the war between the states? Every time I saw that sergeant, I remembered that I was a Southern lady and that right was on my side. And I also had to remember my vow to stay strong. My friends and I had sworn! I tried to ignore my shivering and used the last of my strength to drag myself after Captain Mazer's wagon.

, , ,

"Ma!" Joanna had just finished talking to Captain Mazer. She joined the rest of us as we slowly followed his wagon through the town. "Ma, Captain Mazer has learned that the boat we are to go on will not leave until morning—perhaps not until midday. They are collecting the sick and wounded from the regiments hereabouts, and that is bound to take awhile. Ma, he really is rallying," Joanna said, eyes shining despite the cold and wet.

"He has suggested that we simply take a little detour to the synagogue—the sergeant won't know the difference. With the celebrations for Christmas, which are already beginning, our absence will probably go unnoticed. And if there is a problem, Captain Mazer outranks the sergeant—although since this is apparently not Jonathan's jurisdiction, that could become a little troublesome. So he suggests that we be discreet and that we show up at the docks by daybreak."

"God bless him," Ma answered.

"He's ordered his wagon to drive right past the synagogue—and says you should ride up there with him and David. We'll be there in no time!"

I was so relieved to hear the news that had Captain Mazer himself delivered it, I might have forgotten all my reservations and thrown my arms around his neck in gratitude. He was certainly worthy of some respect for these actions, I had to admit. My teeth were by then chattering so violently that I could think of nothing else but a fire and dry clothes. That would be heaven.

December 25, 1862

When we arrived at the synagogue, evening services had just finished. Since it was the last night of Chanukah, the synagogue had no doubt been filled with people, but most had already left for home. We staggered into the sanctuary like something the cat had dragged in. Rabbi Tuska took one look at us and exclaimed, "My dear Mrs. Green! Children! Oh, what in heaven's name has happened?"

Ma quickly explained.

"I have heard," Rabbi Tuska said, "that the Jews of Paducah were given twenty-four hours to pack and leave town—thirty families forced to flee! But the Union is capable of any kind of evil." He paused. "We must get you dry!"

An older man with a full white beard and gentle brown eyes walked over to us. "Mrs. Green!" He still had a heavy German accent, unlike my parents, who had managed to lose theirs almost completely.

"Oh, Mr. Adler."

"Please, Mrs. Green, Sarah has dinner waiting. And you know we have too many empty rooms with the children all away. Please, come to our home, it is only a five-minute walk, and let us get you and the children dry and fed."

"Thank you, Mr. Adler, we would be so grateful."

"Grateful? No. You would do the same for us. Where is your luggage?"

Ma explained that what little we had had gone ahead to the ship with Captain Mazer.

And so we all walked to Mr. Adler's home, where Mrs. Adler met us at the door. In no time she had her maid drawing hot water for the tub and heating water for footbaths. She had Mr. Adler and the footman take charge of David and Henry, and she herself took charge of Joanna, Ma, and me.

"Clara," Mrs. Adler said, "I never thought to see you in these straits. Honestly, it breaks my heart. How have you held up?"

"I haven't held up at all well," Ma admitted as we climbed the stairs after Mrs. Adler.

"Don't believe her, Mrs. Adler," Joanna interjected. "Why, she's been strong as an ox."

"I feel as stupid as one too," Ma admitted. "I can't help but think that I should have been able to spare my family this suffering."

"It is not you but that terrible order that is at fault," Mrs. Adler assured her. "Now, I suggest the first thing we do is strip you all out of every piece of clothing you have on. I have closets full of underclothes and dresses from my girls—you may choose whatever you like." She hurried us into her boudoir, where a fire was burning cheerfully and a black maid, whom Mrs. Adler called Mary, was already filling a bath with water. Jule had followed us, but Mrs. Adler turned to her and said, "You must get out of those clothes. Go to the kitchen. Someone will show you where you can wash, and they'll give you a clean, dry dress."

"Oh, no," Jule protested. "I couldn't!"

"Jule," Ma said, "if Mrs. Adler has a spare dress, you

take it." She turned to Mrs. Adler. "I will repay all of this as soon as I can!"

"Nonsense," Mrs. Adler replied, "we have things going to waste here. It may be harder to find clothes that fit the boys—most of the extra things we had we sent for the war. They need so much, don't they?" She stopped and looked at me. "Why, Clara, I declare Hannah has turned all blue around the lips. She'd best get in that hot water first."

I was too cold and tired to object. I tried to unbutton my dress myself, but my hands were shaking so violently I couldn't even grasp one of the buttons.

"Dear God, Hannah," Ma said, "I hadn't realized how bad you were." She and Mrs. Adler and the maid began to pull my wet things off me one by one, until they finally had me undressed and could put me in the bath. Normally my modesty would have forbidden anyone to help me, but I was far beyond such niceties at that moment. I sank into the water, teeth still chattering, shaking all over, and it took a full five minutes before I stopped shaking. Mrs. Adler hung my coat, toque, gloves, and dress by the fire and quickly laid out dry ones. They dressed me in a warm wool camp dress with woolen stockings and sat me by the fire. Mrs. Adler wrapped a thick blanket around me and then placed a sweet wine in my hand. "Drink that down," she ordered. I obeyed. And finally I began to feel warm again.

The same ritual was followed by my ma and my sister, until we were all warm, dry, and slightly intoxicated with the wine we were drinking on an empty stomach.

"Now, food!" Mrs. Adler stated. "Follow me. We go straight to the dining room!"

Candles lit the long table, covered in a delicate light yellow lace cloth, and sterling silverware glistened at each place. Mr. Adler and the boys were already seated.

I laughed aloud when I saw Henry and David, surprising myself, as only hours earlier I had thought I would never laugh again. Perhaps it was the wine. Still, the boys did present a comical tableau. Both were in jackets twice their size, sleeves rolled up, collars sticking up past their ears. But they looked clean and dry, and that was all that mattered.

A bean soup was served first, followed by a tender brisket, mashed turnips, stewed pumpkin, and pickled cucumbers. I had to smile as I watched David move his vegetables around so it would look as if he'd eaten them. Hungry as he was, he could not abide turnips. We were all encouraged to drink more wine, this time a thick red one, and I soon began to feel warm, full, and decidedly light-headed. Ma told the Adlers about the loss of our home. And then she and the Adlers spoke of other losses. Mrs. Adler listed all the Jewish boys from the temple who had been killed. We had known all of them. It was heartbreaking news. And of course, the Adlers had lost a son to pneumonia while he was in camp, only six months earlier.

I knew that everyone at our temple looked up to Mr. Adler. He was considered the wisest, most learned man there, perhaps in the entire city of Memphis. Even the rabbis went to him for advice. I was so troubled by the events of the past few days that as I sat there I began to hope that perhaps, if I asked him, he could shed some light on everything that had happened.

"Pardon me, Mr. Adler, but I would so appreciate your thoughts on these troubles. When we hear about all those who have died, well, it is only natural to hate the Union—we *must* hate them. On this trip people have tried to convince me that we in the South are wrong! But everything proves otherwise!"

"Actually, Hannah," Joanna corrected me, "no one has tried to convince you of anything—it is just that you see the injustice done to us as Jews. Perhaps that is making you question the way you think."

Why couldn't Joanna be quiet just for once? Had I asked for her opinion? I wanted to hear Mr. Adler speak. I wanted to hear what *he* would say.

In fact he did speak before I had a chance to snap back at Joanna.

"I perceive that you girls disagree." He thought for a moment. "I understand it is due to the kindness of a Union soldier that you are here in our home."

Joanna nodded, pleased.

"And it is due to Union soldiers that you are in this unfortunate situation," he continued.

I nodded vigorously.

"Children," Mr. Adler said, "there is one thing I can tell you. Hatred is *always* bad. And, Hannah, this I hope you *will* understand. There is a Jewish saying, 'Love blinds us to faults, hatred to virtues.' You cannot believe that the Union is all evil or that the Confederacy is all good. There is an old story: An angel visits a man and tells him he can have any wish in the world. There is only one rule. Whatever he wishes for, his neighbor will receive it and more—double. The man thinks. Above everything in the world, he hates this neighbor. So, in the end, what does he wish for? He says to the angel, 'Make me blind in one eye.' This reminds me of the war we are in now. We will destroy ourselves in order to destroy the others."

This was not the answer I had hoped for. I wanted more than anything in the world, more than being warm or dry or having hot food in my stomach, not to be bothered by troubling thoughts. I wanted Mr. Adler to tell me that my usual way of thinking was correct. He had two boys fighting for the Confederacy. He had lost one already. Surely he saw things clearly.

"We have freed all our slaves," Mrs. Adler added quietly.

There was a moment of stunned silence. I looked at the two who were serving, a Negro man and a Negro girl.

"They are in my employ," Mr. Adler explained. "They all chose to stay after we gave them their papers." Mr. Adler looked at me and spoke sympathetically. "I am sorry you are confused, Hannah," he said. "But I must warn you, everyone will have a different answer for you. Dr. Raphall of New York City wrote a paper showing that the Bible supports slavery and that Jews should too. And Michael Heilprin of Philadelphia, a learned scholar, wrote an answer to it in the *New York Tribune* that was very convincing, showing that the Bible does *not* sanction slavery."

"Captain Mazer gave me that article to read," said Joanna.

"You see, my dears," Mr. Adler said, "there will always be clever people who can give you reasons for taking a certain position—or the opposite position."

"But then, how do you know who is right?" I exclaimed in frustration.

"All of us must decide for ourselves," Mr. Adler answered.

"But how can we?" Joanna asked. "If you are taught to believe *one* thing, how on earth can you change that way of thinking, how can you learn it is wrong? Why, that sergeant will always hate Jews, no matter what!"

"I see that you have changed your thinking, Joanna," Mr. Adler said.

"She is in love," I snorted.

"It is true," Joanna admitted, "that had I not met Captain Mazer, I should probably never have questioned my way of thinking. And that disturbs me."

"In love, love, love . . . ," sang David.

"It was not easy for me at first," Joanna said, "to accept what Jonathan told me. It made me feel like a traitor."

Henry shook his head. "She is confused. *And* a traitor, too. Hannah will have more sense than to think like that!"

"'God does not predetermine whether a man shall be righteous or wicked, that He leaves to man himself,'"

Mr. Adler quoted. "And here let me tell you what I think is the most important command from God: 'Love thy neighbor as thyself. I am God.' And for me," Mr. Adler explained, "for me, the best of us, the love we have in us, *that* is God. Wherever there is love, there is God."

Everyone at the table was silent. I knew that the words he had just spoken were true, the way one simply *knows* something. And yet, if that was the case, why couldn't I just know what the truth was about the war? Why wasn't *it* as clear?

December 26, 1862

I have gone over everything now, in my mind, from ten days ago, until today. And yet, am I any closer to *knowing*, to *understanding*? I keep remembering Mr. Adler's words and feel there is a secret there if only I could grasp it; but my thinking seems to be getting more muddled by the moment. Perhaps that is because I am beginning to feel unwell. I do not want to worry Ma, though, so I am standing a bit apart from her and the others, hoping that the chills and aches I am experiencing will pass. A soldier forced me out of the little corner I had been curled up in as I mulled over the past ten days, so I have to stand. I am supporting myself as best I can by leaning on the railing. At least I am spared my sister's company, as she is in the hold of the ship nursing Captain Mazer, who is apparently making an amazing recovery.

"Hannah?" Ma comes up to me. "Your cheeks are bright red." She puts her hand on my forehead. "Oh, my dear, you are burning with fever. You caught a chill last night!"

I am, in fact, feeling chilled to the bone again, even though my face is burning hot. My mind is in a whirl and my body has started to shake and tremble. I suddenly feel very light-headed indeed.

"Henry!" Ma calls. "Jule. Come here! Miss Hannah needs to lie down." But there seems to be nowhere for me to lie down. The inner recess of the ship is filled with supplies and boxes, and any spare room has stretchers for the wounded and ill. Even the deck is filled with soldiers and supplies.

"Here, Ma," Henry says, "we can lay her on top of these boxes here. I'll put my coat down."

Henry holds me by the shoulders and gently lowers me down.

"Thank you, Henry," I whisper. "You are a good brother. You don't worry me like my sister does."

"Of course I don't," Henry replies. "She's crazy as a loon. You lie here quiet and rest. You rest your mind, too, Hannah."

"All right, Henry," I agree, soothed by his words, while everything around continues to spin. "I will." I close my eyes.

But once my eyes are closed, horrible images begin to appear. Yet I am unable to open my eyes to make them go away. I see Moses weeping, then he is shouting at me; Eugenia lectures me to be strong; Mr. Adler is talking, talking, but no words are coming out of his mouth; Leon is calling my name; Holly Springs is exploding all around me. I must cry out, because I hear my own voice too, and then I am hot and then so cold, and I am walking in the rain and mud; the sergeant is laughing—"Jews! Jews! I will see you dead!"

, , ,

"You drink this, Miss Hannah. Miss Hannah! Now, you done listen to me. You ain't gonna get better if you won't cooperate. You ain't."

"Listen to Jule, Hannah. Drink."

Who is that? Jule *was* talking. Now some man is ordering me. He sounds serious. Perhaps I should listen.

It takes all my strength to open my mouth and swallow. A bitter taste hits my throat along with a searing, burning pain.

"Good, Miss Hannah. Again."

I open my mouth. The pain in my throat the second time I swallow is almost unbearable.

' ' '

I finally manage to get my eyes open. It is dark. I try to speak but my throat is like a burning fire. I feel a cool cloth on my forehead and I hear a man's voice again, but it is so pitch-black I cannot see who it is.

"How is she?"

"Miss Hannah? Miss Hannah?"

Where am I? Where is Pa? Where is my bed, my dear room all yellow and white, sun streaming in, the scent of magnolias . . . where is Ma? I try to call for Ma.

"Hannah, dear, I'm right here. You must drink a little."

I try to shake my head but nothing will move, my muscles will not obey. I can't drink again. I remember that it hurts to drink.

I close my eyes. I can hear voices. Someone is angry. Someone is arguing.

"How can we move her, sir?"

"You will have to, madam."

"Look at her!"

"We are all changing ships. This one turns around and goes back to Memphis. You and your family must continue on."

"They are under my protection." That man again. Pa?

"Then get some of your lads to carry her. She's just a bit of a thing."

"Her brother and her sister will . . ." I can't hear any more. My head hurts so badly I want to cry.

My eyes fly open. A jolt awakens me. My head is pounding. Everything aches, every muscle, every joint in my body. Henry and Joanna are carrying me. Why? Where are we going? Every step they take jars my back. The pain is so terrible I want to scream, but my burning throat won't allow it. I close my eyes and grit my teeth.

, , ,

I must have lost consciousness. I look around. I am sitting in an office, on a hard wooden bench, held up by Henry. Jule is on my other side, coaxing me to drink something. Captain Mazer stands over me. He is ordering me to drink. He reminds me of Pa somehow. I know I'd better listen to him. I drink what Jule gives me.

Ma is sitting in a chair across from a little gray-haired man with big, bushy eyebrows who sits behind a huge wooden desk.

"Now, Mrs. Green," he says, "there you go, passports all in order. These papers will let you travel safely anywhere in the Union—outside of General Grant's jurisdiction. I understand you are to go on a boat to Cincinnati."

"Yes," Ma answers.

"I did the papers for the families from Paducah. They had a delegation going to see the president himself. I've heard this order won't stand, ma'am. Why, you'll be home in no time, I'm sure."

I wish I were a man. They are all liars, those Yanks. I should be a man. I should kill all of them! I should . . . Where is my room? Where is Leon? Where am I? Simon knows everything. Simon should be here. He could tell me where I am.

' ' '

I am in a carriage in a strange town and Captain Mazer is my pa. He is taking care of me. And Jule is my ma. She is nursing me. No, that couldn't be right. I have a different pa and a different ma.

Jule and Henry carry me up a gangplank onto a ship and lay me down. It is so noisy. Where is my dear room? Where is Joanna? Oh, there she is—but she's turned into a big, fierce bobcat. The cat is going to scratch me. Joanna is scaring me. Why is she being so cruel?

' ' '

"Drink."

I am wet. Am I swimming? I love to swim with my friends. Only we have to be careful of the snakes. And the mosquitoes, because Ma doesn't want me to catch malaria. Why am I wet? Why do they make me drink? Someone is crying. Is it Leon? I need to go help Leon. He is sick. He's been captured. I have to get up, but I can't move. I can't even open my eyes.

' ' '

"Hannah, you must forgive me. I was cruel to you. Hannah, please forgive me."

What is the matter with Joanna? Oh, now I remember. She has turned into a bobcat. That *is* cruel. Well, I shall not forgive her. Some things are beyond forgiveness. A bobcat! What could she be thinking?

, , ,

"I never goes anywheres without my potions." It sounds like Jule talking. Is Jule, after all, a witch? "My ma, she'd slap me to tomorrow if I done travel without them. 'There's always people who'll need 'em,' she'd say. 'And it's our duty to help 'em. Cuz we knows how. Those doctors, they just ignorant.' What cures a fever?"

"Bleeding." Is that Pa?

"No, that done make you weaker! It willow bark for sure! Mixed with osha and some other herbs. It's an old Indian cure!"

I try to open my eyes, but they feel like someone has glued them shut. I cannot get them open. I want to tell someone. Ma! I have to tell Ma. I hear my voice croak Ma's name.

"Hannah, it's Ma. Hannah. Can you open your eyes?"

That's the problem! I can't.

"Missus, let me wash her eyes." It is Jule. "Miss Hannah, your eyes be infected, and it's keepin' 'em shut. Missus, I got some goldenseal here. I gonna make it into a wash and clean out her eyes. It should work after a few times."

"Hannah," Ma says, "don't worry. Jule is going to clean your eyes so you can open them. I know it's frightening, but relax now. Imagine you are in your bed at home and the birds are singing outside your window.

And later in the day you and your friends are going to play at cards."

No, there's no time for cards. I have to help in the store. Ma needs my help. Mrs. Clemens is bringing her fresh pies in for us to sell, and I have to keep David away from the cherry ones. I have to check the butter and sort the eggs for Mr. Fisher. Mr. Lewis will want me to measure out his beer from the keg. Mrs. Hunter is sending Eugenia to buy a paint set for her little sister, and Mary is coming in to smell the perfumes. I'd best get up. I have so much to do.

"Hannah, lie back, child." It is that man again. Pa?

I lie back. Pa always knows what to do. He'll be busy showing Mr. Ellis that new saddle that just came in. Where's Moses? Jimmy Jones wants a new pair of boots, and Moses can fit anyone up perfect each time. And Moses knows the guns, too. So why is he shooting the customers? Tell Moses to stop shooting the customers!

"Hannah, Ma is here. Don't cry, sweetheart. Don't cry. You lie there peaceful."

"Shouldn't have reminded her of home, it's made her remember." The bobcat is talking. "Hannah, remember the prayers Pa taught us? I want you to say them with me, Hannah. We need to pray to God now to help us. God will help us, Hannah. You say it inside your head, I'll say it aloud."

"Hear Israel! God is our Lord, God is One! Praised be the glorious name of His Kingdom, for evermore."

It is funny to hear a cat praying to God. But it makes

her seem less scary. I have to giggle a little. A cat praying *is* funny. And now she is singing.

> "Adon olam, asher malach
> Beterem kol yetsir nivra
> leeit naasa vecheftsokol
> azai melech shemo nikra."

I love that melody. I remember it from services. We always sang it. It makes me feel happy . . . and peaceful.

I awake to singing. Eyes still closed, I can hear sweet voices:

> "I awake my soul and with the sun
> The daily course of duty run;
> Shake off dull sloth, an early rise
> To pay thy memory sacrifice.

> "Glory to thee, who safe has kept,
> and hast refreshed me while I sleep;
> Grant, Lord, when I from death shall wake,
> I may of endless life partake."

Over the top of the singing I hear what sounds like two people arguing.

"You are crazy, girl. You best leave now when you can. Once you're back in Mississippi, you won't be able to escape!" It is a man's voice, very deep. And gentle too, although he obviously is desperate to be convincing.

"But I don't want to leave 'em. You don't understand. The master took me away from a terrible place. Terrible. I would've died there, sure."

"And you've saved his daughter, haven't you? So you're even. A life for a life."

His daughter? With a shock I suddenly realize that I am listening to Jule and someone else and the daughter must mean me. I open my eyes a mite and see a tall, young Negro man crouched beside Jule, staring into her eyes with an almost fierce intensity.

"But where would I go? What would I do? They take good care of me. I got no skills—can't read or write. I know how girls like me end up."

"You tell me they've lost their house and their shop."

"Yes."

"So now they'll need money. How do you make quick money? You sell your possessions." Then he stared at her for a moment until his words sunk in.

"Me?"

"Yes, you! And they could sell you to someone just as mean as mean could be."

I don't want it to happen, but a small groan escapes my throat. Quickly the young man gets up and leaves. Jule bends over me. I look up at her and feel like I am seeing her for the first time—and I am shocked to notice how pretty she is. Her face is round, she has full lips, a small nose, and large black eyes. Why, that young man is obviously sweet on her. Jule smiles at me.

"I tol' your ma you'd be fine. I may be clumsy at most things, Miss Hannah, but I's got a knack for curing and illness. Got it from my ma. She took care of all the slaves. She knows every potion there is. . . . Look at your eyes, all cleared up now. Fever broke. . . . I'll go get your ma."

Ma, face pale and drawn, is soon leaning over me. "Hannah! Sweet child! We thought we'd lose you for certain." She starts to weep as she bends to kiss my forehead. "Jule had seen this kind of fever before. . . . If not for her . . ."

So it is true what I just overheard. Jule has saved my life.

I notice a foul odor then, and I try to raise myself up to see where I am, but I am too weak. "Ma? Where are we? What's happened? I'm thirsty."

Ma holds my head up and gives me a small drink of tepid water out of a tin cup. "We are on a hospital boat run by the Sanitary Commission," she answers. "We've just passed Paducah. You were delirious all day yesterday. We stopped in Cairo, where they issued our passports, and got onto this ship. Joanna, Jule, and Henry took turns carrying you. Do you remember any of it?"

"It's all like a strange dream," I say, my voice still very weak. But at least my throat no longer feels like it is on fire. It is sore, but much better.

I manage to raise my head just a bit and look around. I am in the hold of a ship, crowded with stretchers, all soldiers who are obviously sick or wounded. There are also many Negroes who are tending them. It must have been the Negroes I heard singing the morning hymn when I first awakened. One or two continue to sing as they work.

Captain Mazer kneels beside me. "Hannah, are you feeling better?"

That voice. I remember that voice. I thought it was Pa.

"Pa?" I ask, wondering if perhaps he *is* there.

"No, Hannah, you mistook me for your pa in your illness. Which was a great compliment to me," he adds.

"You would listen only to Captain Mazer," Ma says, smiling. "Without him we could not have gotten a thing down you."

He takes my hand. "I am sorry, Hannah, that I am not your pa. But I am very glad you listened to me. And I am overjoyed to see you so improved."

I have no more strength left in me to hate him. The grip of his hand feels strong and reassuring, and I am thankful he is here and that we are under his protection. The fact that I do not pull away from him seems enough of a thanks for him and he smiles. "You must close your eyes and rest now. Your sister is busy nursing—there are a thousand sick soldiers on this ship and much work to be done."

I close my eyes. All around me I can hear the groans and sighs of the ill, mixed in with the Negroes' singing.

That hymn I woke to, it reminds me so much of something. And suddenly I remember the hymn we always sang at services at the temple in Memphis—"Adon Olam." I have read the English translation in the prayer book so often that I know it by heart. How similar the words of the hymns are.

> *Into His hands I entrust my spirit, when I sleep and when*
> *I wake; and with my spirit, my body also; the Lord is*
> *with me, I will not fear.*

Had Joanna sung it to me earlier?

And then with a jolt I recall that it is Federals lying all around me, Federals and Negroes singing of God. Is their God the same as mine? Could Joanna be right after all? And what about the conversation I just overheard? Why, Jule's new friend is correct. Pa *may* have to sell Jule. A shudder runs through me.

"Hannah, are you all right?" Captain Mazer still holds my hand reassuringly in his.

"I just realized something," I whisper. "Jule *is* no different than a horse. Just like Moses said. I understand what he meant. Now I understand."

"Hannah, you must not get yourself upset," Captain Mazer orders me. "You may do your deep thinking when you are well and not before. Is that understood?"

I nod.

"Good. Now, you close your eyes and go back to sleep. We cannot have you relapsing. You must rest."

I am too weak to resist his instruction. I close my eyes and sleep.

, , ,

I still feel weak when I wake up the second time, but my head seems clearer. The tune of "Adon Olam" keeps running through my mind. I turn my head to see Joanna sitting next to me.

"Hannah," she says, "I am so sorry. We thought you might die. I couldn't bear it if anything happened to you—and if you had gone while we were angry at each other . . . we must vow never to be angry again!"

This statement evokes a weak smile from me. "We can vow," I answer softly, "but I doubt that we could hold to such a vow."

Joanna smiles. "Perhaps you are right, little sister."

"Captain Mazer appears to be a good man," I say.

"Has your fever affected your brain?" Joanna chides me. "What has brought about this change of heart?"

"I know that he nursed me. As did Jule. Perhaps they saved my life. Mr. Adler made me wonder . . . and hearing that hymn . . . or maybe I dreamed that. . . ." I pause. "If we are all part of one God, Joanna," I say, "maybe we are all . . . the same. I know I am the same as Eugenia. Maybe Captain Mazer, even though he is Union, is also a creature of God, as you say. And Jule as well . . ."

Joanna takes my hand. "It is simple, my dear. Of course some people will always be richer or more powerful than others. Some will be poor and they will always be treated as lesser. . . . That is the way of the world. But as a class— we Jews cannot be accused as a class and neither can the Negroes."

"But my friends—they will never accept such a thing. They will never accept *me* if I should change my views."

"If they are true friends," Joanna says, "they will continue to love you. Look at the Lewis family. They freed all their slaves last year and they are still accepted into society."

"But I cannot marry Robert, then," I murmur. "He doesn't see wrong in beating his slaves to their death. And Mary will be so disappointed."

Joanna pats my hand. "What kind of man would condone such a thing? Pa would not."

"Perhaps this is my illness talking," I say. "Perhaps I won't feel this way when I recover. I am weak now, and not thinking clearly."

"Or perhaps, in your weakened state, your mind has let down its defenses and allowed some new ideas to enter.

Sometimes I think our minds are like prisons and we are trapped there without even realizing it. How difficult it is to do as Mr. Adler advises and to think for ourselves," Joanna muses.

"And how difficult it is to know who to believe," I sigh. "But I will always remember his admonition—'Love thy neighbor as thyself.' It seems *that* is a good rule to keep in mind at all times."

"Hannah!" Henry squats down beside me. "Hannah, are you better?"

"Much better, Henry, thank you. And how are you?"

"It is torture being on this ship, Hannah! Torture. Why, there are freed slaves everywhere and they behave with no respect! And as for those soldiers, I am sad to see their suffering, but if they would stop fighting they could end ours, too!"

I open my mouth to correct Henry, then close it again. It would take more strength than I possess at this moment to argue with him, and I doubt that my words would change him anyway. After all, it has not been Joanna's words that have changed my view of things, rather everything that has happened to me and my family. It does not seem to have affected Henry in the same way at all. And who knows if the painful changes taking place in me are for the best. I can only *hope* they are.

"Hannah." David runs up to me. "Hannah, you scared us all!" he says, his voice accusing.

"I am sorry, David," I say. "I hope you did not take advantage of my illness to go into my things. My diary, for instance?"

"That was a nasty note you wrote in there!" David exclaims. "You shouldn't say such things to your brother."

I shake my head ever so slightly. "I knew you would not be able to resist reading it once you had started."

Joanna laughs. "Why, David, even at age seven you are too predictable."

I close my eyes. *If only,* I think, *what happens to us in life could be as predictable as the way we will react to it! What,* I wonder, *will be in store for us next?*

Jule hurries up behind David.

"Master David," she scolds, "don't you go running off like that! I didn't know where you got to!"

I look up at Jule. "Thank you, Jule," I say, "for nursing me."

Jule smiles. "You're welcome, Miss Hannah."

"And, Jule?"

"Yes, Miss Hannah?"

"I believe that young man is right. You must obtain a promise from my ma that you will not be sold, or you should leave us now while you can."

There is a complete silence after the words leave my mouth. And then everyone begins talking at once.

"Are you mad, Hannah?" That is Henry.

"I don't understand," Ma says.

"You are quite capable of the most surprising behavior," Joanna chimes in.

And then Jule speaks. "Thank you, Miss Hannah. That is friendly advice."

I nod, satisfied. And then I close my eyes and, with my family around me, fall into a sweet sleep.

"Hannah! Hannah!"

Henry bursts into the back parlor, where I have been forced to lie down so I can rest, Ma convinced I am still weak from my recent illness.

"It's Pa, Hannah! Pa is *here*!"

I throw off the rug that has been placed carefully over my legs and leap to my feet. Just then Pa strides into the room. In a heartbeat I am in his arms, weeping with joy.

"There, there, little darling," Pa says, trying to soothe me. "I'm here now."

He holds me at arm's length and looks at me closely. "You are far too thin," he says, concern in his voice.

"I'm fine, Pa, really I am. You are the one who looks too thin!"

I gaze at his face, which is long and lean in the best of times, but now I notice how the bones in his cheeks stand out, and how his thick black hair is showing some gray. He has dark circles under his deep blue eyes. But his big smile is the same as always.

"Does Ma know you are here?" I ask.

"I may be a fool," Pa says, grinning, "but not so big a fool that I didn't go find your ma first."

"And he was coming out of the front room," Henry says, "when I ran into him! I'll go over to Captain Mazer's to fetch Joanna, Pa."

Ma comes into the parlor then, beaming. "I'm organizing some tea, dear," she says. "You sit down and visit with Hannah."

Pa sits in a high-backed chair and motions for me to sit back on the sofa. He gets up and tucks the rug around me, then sits down again.

"What is the news, Pa?"

"Let us wait until the family is together," Pa suggests. "In the meantime, you tell me your news."

"My news is that if I have to stay in this house one more day, I'll become crazed," I say, lowering my voice so only Pa can hear me. "My cousin Miriam is by far the most difficult person I have ever met."

It seems to me I can see a small smile flit across Pa's face. "Pa!" I exclaim. "*I* am not difficult!"

"Of course you are not," Pa says, trying to look serious. "What is the matter with Miriam?"

"I . . . well, I cannot discuss it with you," I reply. Seeing the hurt look on his face, I feel I must explain. "It is women's concerns."

How can I tell him that although Miriam is my age, she has been wearing a corset for a year now and has developed a seventeen inch waist, which is still shrinking? Every week my aunt pulls the laces tighter. And Miriam turns up her nose at me, treating me as if I am some kind of country bumpkin. Me, the epitome of a Southern lady! And to make it worse, Miriam has no manners! Why, *she* is no lady, no lady at all! And Ma will hear no talk of corsets until my fourteenth birthday.

"The boys are impossible," I continue. "David and Reuben race about the house all day playing war games, tumbling in and out of rooms, pretending to be shooting whatever moves. As for my older cousins, Rachel and

Sarah, they take every opportunity to lecture me on how evil the South is, or how we aren't good Jews because we don't observe the Sabbath and keep kosher or attend an Orthodox synagogue as they do." I look at him. "Pa, the order has been revoked, so when can we go home?"

Just then David explodes into the room, throwing himself at Pa with such strength that the chair Pa is in almost tips over backward. "Pa, Pa, Pa," he screams, again and again. Following close behind him is Joanna, who also falls into Pa's arms. Finally Ma comes in, followed by Jule, who is carrying a tray with tea and cakes on it.

When David sees Jule, he exclaims to Pa, "Jule's been emancemated!"

"Emancipated," I correct him with a smile. "You heard, didn't you, Pa, that all slaves in the Confederate states are declared free by President Lincoln?"

"Of course I heard, Hannah. But you have chosen to stay with us, Jule?"

"I wouldn't leave for the whole world, Master Green. You practically saved my life."

"Jule *did* save Hannah," Joanna says.

"How?" Pa asks.

Everyone talks at once then, trying to tell Pa about what happened to us. When we have more or less gotten him caught up, there is an expectant silence as we wait for his reaction.

"You have each one of you been brave and strong," he declares. "I cannot tell you how proud I am of all of you." And he throws Ma a special kind of look. He pauses for a minute before speaking again. "When I arrived in Holly Springs and found you all gone, I could think of only one thing. Were you all healthy, were you all alive? I didn't care about the house, I didn't care about the store. Those are only things. I traveled here in the hope that you would have come to my brother, and you did. When I walked into this house and saw your ma and she told me you were all here and you were all well, it was the happiest moment of my life." A tear trickles down his cheek. "We will go back to Holly Springs now that this despicable order has been revoked. When I left there, it looked like Grant was planning to leave. We'll start up the shop again. We can build a small home where the old one used to stand, for now. It won't be easy, but I think it is best that we return."

Relief overwhelms me when I hear those words.

"One more thing. I have heard from a good source that the group of prisoners Leon is with is to be paroled, perhaps have already been paroled. I want us to be home for Leon." He bites his lip before he speaks again. "I was also told that there has been an outbreak of smallpox in the prison at Alton, where I believe Leon was taken. Many boys are in quarantine. I tried to find out more but was unable to. Either Leon will come home, or we will hear news of him. . . . Yes, we must return," he repeats.

I am overcome by joy and fear at the same time. Perhaps my prayers are about to be answered. On the other hand, I know that there is no guarantee that Leon will be with the paroled group. What if his illness overpowered him and he is already with God? Or what if he has succumbed to the outbreak of smallpox?

Ma is crying quietly. "If anyone has the strength to make it home, it must be Leon," she says, half as a prayer, half as a description of how strong Leon has always proved to be.

"Ma," Joanna says, "have you told Pa?"

"Joanna will not be going with us," Ma says as she dabs at her eyes with a handkerchief. "I imagine she'll stay here with your brother, until she is married."

Joanna looks anxiously at Pa. "He wanted to speak to you, Pa. He wanted to do it properly."

"He still can. Tell him to come see me later," Pa says. "I understand from your ma's letters that he is a lovely man. For a Yank."

Joanna smiles. "For a Yank," she agrees.

January 15, 1863

"'How are we then to love God in our neighbor?'"

Pa is reading from *The Catechism for Jewish Children*. He was thrilled that I had chosen to save it of all things, and told me the choice showed me to be a person of substance, rather than a frivolous young girl. We are on the deck of the steamer that is taking us back to Memphis. Both of us are perched on a large wooden crate, the only seat we could find.

"Mr. Adler said we should love our neighbor as ourselves," I reply.

"Correct," Pa agrees. "The catechism says, 'We should honor in our neighbor the image of God and look upon him as our equal and brother, though he may be subject to our control for the present; for the time will come when death will render us all equal again—'"

"Pa," I interrupt, "did you ever feel that owning slaves was wrong?"

Pa sits very still for a moment, thinking before he answers. "To be honest, Hannah, I never gave it much thought. We arrived here from the old country and all I really wanted was to be accepted by our new neighbors. It was so bad in the old country, being hated simply because we were Jews. I had never seen a colored person before arriving in America. When my new friends made it clear that Negroes were our inferiors and that owning them was a sign that we were part of society, why, I just fell right in with it."

"But Moses was very clever and good," I say. "Didn't

he make you wonder sometimes if you should own him?"

"I never thought about it," Pa admitted. "Perhaps I did not want to make our lives any more complicated by going against everyone. To tell you the truth, I'm sure my views would have remained the same if it had not been for General Grant's order against all Jews. I realized how similar our situation was to the Negroes'." He pauses for another minute. "Hannah, I am afraid I set you a bad example. I did not do the right thing because I did not want any trouble. That is not a very brave or noble reason for one's actions."

Pa continues to read from the catechism. "'Have we not all one Father? Hath not one God created us? Why do we deal treacherously every man against his brother, to profane the covenant of our fathers? Malachi, chapter two, verse ten.'"

"I'm afraid to go back, Pa," I say quietly. "For all the reasons you just said. I'm afraid my friends will only see me as a Jew after this order. And when they find my views have changed, and that Jule is free . . . we all know that they will pay no attention at all to the Emancipation Proclamation. . . ." My voice trails off.

"I am afraid of the same thing," Pa admits. "I hope we can still have a good life there. But if we cannot, Hannah, we still have our family. Even Henry, who loves us dearly despite believing we have lost our minds."

He hugs me. It seems that the order and certainty I have lived for is gone forever. I will have to learn to live with the knowledge that life will most probably always be unpredictable. I hope I can learn how to be happy in that knowledge.

"Don't worry, Hannah," Pa says with a smile, seeming to sense my thoughts. "You will always be a Southern lady, no matter where we end up."

"Will I, Pa?"

"You will. Now, here is the next question in the catechism."

And we bend our heads together and continue to study.

Afterword

> General Orders No. 11
>
> The Jews, as a class violating every regulation of trade established by the Treasury Department and also department orders, are hereby expelled from the department within twenty-four hours from the receipt of this order.
>
> Post commanders will see that all of this class of people be furnished passes and required to leave, and any-one returning after such notification will be arrested and held in confinement until an opportunity occurs of sending them out as prisoners, unless furnished with permit from headquarters.
>
> No passes will be given these people to visit head-quarters for the purpose of making personal application for trade permits.
>
> By order of Maj. Gen. U. S. Grant
>
> JNO. A. RAWLENS,
> Assistant Adjutant General

, , ,

This was the order that caused the Jewish people so much anguish. Their sons were fighting and dying for the Union, and yet they were being treated with con-tempt. Thirty families in Paducah, Kentucky, were forced from their homes, as well as families and individu-als from Mississippi. Here is part of the letter written to President Lincoln from the leaders of the Jewish commu-nity in Paducah.

Padukah, Kentucky
December 29, 1862

Hon. ABRAHAM LINCOLN,
President of the United States

General Orders, No. 11, issued by General Grant at Oxford, Miss., December the 17th, commands all post commanders to expel all Jews, without distinction, within twenty-four hours, from his entire department. The undersigned, good and loyal citizens of the United States and residents of this town for many years, engaged in legitimate business as merchants, feel greatly insulted and outraged by this inhuman order, the carrying out of which would be the grossest violation of the Constitution and our rights as good citizens under it, and would place us, besides a large number of other Jewish families of this town, as outlaws before the whole world. We respectfully ask your immediate attention to this enormous outrage on all law and humanity, and pray for your effectual and immediate interposition.

D. WOLFF & BROS.
C. F. KASKEL
J. W. KASKEL

Cesar Kaskel then traveled to Washington and gained access to the president. Their conversation was reported to have gone like this:

LINCOLN: *And so the children of Israel were driven
   from the happy land of Canaan?*
KASKEL: *Yes, and that is why we have come unto
   Father Abraham's bosom, asking protection.*
LINCOLN: *And this protection they shall have at once.*

On January 7, 1863, U. S. Grant revoked General Orders No.11, and Jews who had been driven from their homes were allowed to return. For anyone wishing to read more about this I recommend *American Jewry and the Civil War* by Bertram W. Korn.

A note about the Reform movement in America at that time: The seeds of the Reform movement were laid down in the 1750s. The German philosopher Moses Mendelssohn (1729–1786), one of the movement's first great religious leaders, argued that Jews could live modern lives without being false to their religion. Followers of Reform Judaism didn't believe in following all the traditional rules laid down in Orthodox Judaism. Hannah's family is dedicated to its Judaism. They learned to read Hebrew so they can follow the service, although increasingly in those days the service in a Reform temple was mostly in English or in the language of the country of the immigrants, often German. The catechism Hannah's family studies was actually written by a traditional Jewish rabbi, but he modeled it on an older one written by Edward Kley, a German Reform rabbi, so it was widely used by all Jews at the time.

The translations of prayers are from a Reform siddur published in 1863. Although this publication date is slightly later than my story, the prayers would have been in common use well before they were published.

Readers often ask if I base my characters on one particular person from history. The answer is no. I do extensive research and try hard to make the book as historically accurate *as possible,* but I always remind my readers that this is a work, first and foremost, of fiction. The characters are my creations plunked down in a historical setting.